# In a Deserted Steam Tunnel

"Doesn't look like anybody's been down here in a while," Joe said, and kept walking. "At least there are no monsters."

"Joe, look out!"

Frank rushed forward, but he was too late. Joe had already tripped on a thin strand of wire strung across the corridor a few inches above the floor. Frank grabbed Joe's shirt to try to keep him from falling, but Joe's momentum pulled his brother down with him. Instead of hitting the cement floor of the tunnel, Joe and Frank landed on soft netting.

"Boy," Joe said, "lucky this net was here."

"Maybe not so lucky," Frank replied. "I'm stuck."

"Hey, me, too!" Joe said. Sure enough, the sticky strands of the netting held them tight.

"Joe, this isn't a net," Frank said. "It's a giant spiderweb!"

# THE **HARDY BOYS**®

## A GAME CALLED CHAOS

FRANKLIN W. DIXON

## SCHOLASTIC INC.

New York  Toronto  London  Auckland  Sydney
Mexico City  New Delhi  Hong Kong  Buenos Aires

This book is a work of fiction. Any references to historical events, real people, or real locales are used fictitiously. Other names, characters, places, and incidents are the product of the author's imagination, and any resemblance to actual events or locales or persons, living or dead, is entirely coincidental.

Copyright © 2000 Simon & Schuster, Inc.

ISBN 0-7172-6946-9

Printed in the U.S.A.
First Scholastic printing, March 2004

# Contents

# A GAME CALLED CHAOS

# 1 Cousins in Chaos

"My cousin Chelsea is in trouble," Phil Cohen said on a bright, sunny summer morning. He stood in the Hardys' front yard, frowning and rubbing his chin with his thin fingers.

Joe Hardy glanced at his older brother, Frank. They'd been friends with Phil a long time and knew him well. When Phil rubbed his chin, it didn't just mean trouble, it meant *big* trouble, the kind that even brainy Phil couldn't think his way out of.

Joe bobbed his head toward the front door of the house. "Come on in, Phil," he said. "We can talk about it over some breakfast."

Phil shook his head. "I don't have much time," he said. "I'm in the middle of a project, and I

1

have to get back to work." Phil had parlayed his skill with computers into a number of high-paying part-time jobs. Joe figured he must be working on a tight deadline.

"Don't keep us guessing, Phil," Frank said. "We can't help if we don't know what the trouble is."

"Well," Phil said, "Chelsea's a project manager at Viking Software up in Jewel Ridge, Connecticut."

"Viking . . . That's a new company, isn't it?" Joe asked. "I think I read something about it in *E-Gaming* magazine. Didn't they put out that Norseman's Revenge shareware game?"

"Yeah, they've released a couple of pretty good games. Nothing to really put them on the map yet, though," Phil said. "But the project Chelsea's working on could change all that. Have you ever heard of the Chaos series?"

"Heard of it?" Joe said, smiling broadly. "Caverns of Chaos is just about my favorite computer game ever."

"I could hardly get any computer time to write my American history term paper," Frank said. "Joe wouldn't give up the computer."

"Hey, that's all ancient history now," Joe said with a laugh. "Besides, you got an A on that paper." He turned back to Phil. "So, what's the Chaos series got to do with your cousin?"

"Well, her company is putting out the next

game in the series. But she, well . . . she told me she's lost the guy who's writing the game."

"Steven Royal?" Joe asked.

"Yeah, that's his name," Phil replied.

"How do you lose a computer game designer?" Frank asked.

"She'd have to fill you in on the details," said Phil. "I figured something like this is more up your alley than mine. Can you guys help? She told me that if she doesn't find Royal, her job is toast."

"No problema," Joe said, clapping Phil on the shoulder. "We've found a few missing people in our lives. Where do we start looking?"

Two hours later Joe pulled the Hardys' van off the highway and into the outskirts of Jewel Ridge, Connecticut. The town was a former factory town that had caught the high-tech rocket and was riding it to new wealth. As Joe followed Phil's directions to his cousin's office, the Hardys noted that many of the buildings they passed were either brand-new or newly renovated.

"Looks like a nice place to live," Joe said.

"If you can afford it," Frank noted. "Too bad Phil couldn't come along."

"Well, when you've got to work, you've got to work," Joe said. "He said he'd be available by phone if we need him. And maybe he can come up later this weekend."

It didn't take long for the Hardys to find the offices of Viking Software. The company was located in a new building in a small industrial park on the edge of town. The site was beautiful, surrounded by a forest, and even had trees separating the sections of the parking lot. The developer of the building had obviously taken care to blend his work with the existing landscape.

Joe and Frank drove their van into the lot, found a space, and got out. The building itself was ultra-modern, the exterior all steel and mirrored glass, in which the beauty of the natural landscape was reflected. The brothers walked down a short path to the building. A sign in the lobby directed them to the offices of Viking Software, which commanded the entire second floor.

"Hi. We're Frank and Joe Hardy," Frank announced as they approached the reception desk. "Chelsea Sirkin's expecting us."

The receptionist, seated behind a modular gray desk, checked her appointment book. The tag on her lapel said her name was Jeanne. "Yes," she confirmed, smiling brightly. "Ms. Sirkin said to send you right back. She's the third office on your left, near the far wall."

"Thanks, Jeanne," Joe said, returning her smile.

Chelsea Sirkin met the Hardys halfway between the reception desk and her office. Frank and Joe figured the receptionist must have buzzed her when they came in. Chelsea was a short, thin young woman about twenty years old, with frizzy blond hair and round glasses.

"Hi," she said, extending her hand. "I'm so glad you could come. We're almost frantic about this whole thing. Dave Henderson, my boss, is pacing his office like a caged tiger."

"We'll do what we can," Frank said. "But first, you'd better fill us in on everything."

"Okay," Chelsea said. "Let's go into my office. Would either of you like a soda?"

"Sure," Joe said.

"Whatever you've got," added Frank.

Chelsea stopped at the staff lunchroom and grabbed three colas out of the fridge. "You might want to take some chairs," she said. "I don't have any extras in my office."

She held the drinks while the brothers each hauled a chair down the hall to Chelsea's office.

As he entered the office, Joe decided he'd seldom seen such a mess in his life. Papers lay scattered about everywhere, overflowing from Chelsea's desk to the floor. Some looked like memos, others had designs for video game characters on them. Posters from movies and video games decorated the walls. A tower of books almost high enough to tumble over lay on a single shelf attached to one wall. The opposite wall was made entirely of glass and looked out over the parking lot.

"Sorry about the mess," Chelsea said sheepishly, "but, as I said, things have been pretty crazy around here."

"Phil said you 'lost' your game designer?" Frank said.

Chelsea rubbed her chin in a way that reminded the Hardys of Phil. "I think so," she said. "But I'm not really sure. Steven Royal has always been eccentric—we knew that even before we hired him. He's been designing A Town Called Chaos, which will be the fourth game in the Chaos series."

"I thought there was just one game," Frank said.

"You need to get out more often," Joe said, grinning at his older brother. "He did School of Chaos after the first one. It was an even bigger hit—I just didn't hog as much computer time with it. There was a third one, too, but I never bought it."

"Yes," Chelsea said, "Forest of Chaos didn't do as well. I think that's part of the reason Royal left his old publishers. But his new game is fabulous. We're lucky to have him aboard. That is, we would be, if we could find him."

"Have you contacted the police?" Joe asked.

"We've talked to them, yes," Chelsea said, "but

6

Royal . . . well, he's got a reputation as an eccentric. His car is gone and the police are pretty sure Steven's just taking an unannounced vacation."

"What makes you think he isn't?" Frank asked.

"Our production deadline on the game is two weeks away," Chelsea said, "and he hasn't delivered a final version to us. Without it, the game won't get into stores in time for its release date."

"I thought you said it was a great game," Joe said. "How do you know that if you don't have a final copy?"

"We've got a demo version of the first level that we've been giving away on the Internet," Chelsea said. "Plus, Royal showed me the whole game when I visited him at his condo last week. He said he just needed to put in the final touches. It is an amazing game—it has everything, from the usual rolling boulders to a giant ape. Kids are going to love it, and adults, too.

"A Town Called Chaos will prove that Royal's work is state-of-the-art in computer gaming. He said so himself when I saw him. He was real hyped about it. But since then"—she turned her hands palm up—"nothing. He doesn't answer calls or knocks on his door. No one has seen him—and the police don't believe he's really missing." Her eyes misted up a bit, and her lower lip was trembling as she finished.

Joe put a hand on her shoulder. "Don't worry. We believe you, Chelsea," he said in a comforting voice.

"It's not just *my* job," she said, regaining her composure, "it's the future of our whole company. We put most of our start-up money into signing Royal. If this game doesn't come out on time, we won't have enough cash from our other projects to stay afloat. Dave won't even have the chance to fire me because he'll be out of a job, too."

"I think we can help," Frank said. "We're good at tracking things down. Do you think Royal would have gone back to his previous publisher?"

"Wondersoft?" Chelsea asked. "I don't think so. He has a contract with us, and like I said, he wasn't happy with the way their head guy, Ron Rosenberg, promoted Forest of Chaos."

"That's one angle to check out, anyway," Frank said.

"Is there anything else we should know?" Joe asked.

"Yes," Chelsea said. "I meant to mention it earlier." She rummaged around her desk for a moment and came up with a piece of paper. "Yesterday, this e-mail appeared in the mailboxes of everyone at the company. We're pretty sure it's from Royal even though it came from a fake e-mail address." She handed the paper to Frank.

8

*My past is the key to the future. You*
*seek the Town Called Chaos to win the ga*
*The King is waiting. Pawns make the fi*
*move.*

Frank handed the note to Joe.

After a moment Joe said, "The reference to 'King' is probably a word play on Royal's own name."

"Which would make the rest of us the pawns," Frank said. He frowned. "Looks like he wants your company to solve his riddles to find the prototype video game."

"That's what we came up with, too. Royal loves puzzles and riddles—the Chaos series is full of them. Dave is convinced that Royal is using this as a ploy to get more money. But we're tapped out. It's going to be a struggle just to survive until money from Town starts coming in—assuming the game comes out at all. If we had the money, Dave would have hired a professional private investigator to track Royal down."

Joe crossed his arms over his broad chest. "Good thing we Hardys work for soda and burgers."

"For relatives of friends, anyway," Frank added, smiling. "You know, the reference to Royal's past could be to his former publisher, Rosenberg."

9

"So is that our first stop?" Joe asked.

"No," Frank said. "I want to check out Royal's condo first. There might be clues there, or at least something that'll give us a lead on how to approach Rosenberg. Chelsea, I need two things: first, a picture of Royal, so we know who we're looking for."

Chelsea nodded, reached over to a shelf, and pulled off a book. The cover read *Strategy Guide to Caverns of Chaos*. On the back was a photograph of a smiling man and woman. The man appeared to be of medium height and build and had a full beard and long brown hair. The woman was thin and athletic looking and had black hair and green eyes. The man was smiling and the woman looked like a real-life version of Katherine Chaos, the game's heroine. The character Chaos was depicted on the front of the book, dodging flying bats.

"Royal's the man in the picture," Chelsea said.

Frank nodded. "Okay, the second thing we need is directions to Royal's place."

"I can do better than that," Chelsea said. "I'll take you there myself."

"Don't you have work to do?" Joe asked.

Chelsea shrugged sadly. "As Dave said at our staff meeting this morning, if we don't find Royal soon, we're done."

✿　✿　✿

Fifteen minutes later the trio pulled into the parking lot beside Royal's building, which was built along a river. Joe and Frank could see that the place had once been a factory, but extensive renovations had transformed it into a high-priced condo complex. It was three stories high and Chelsea told them it had four units on each floor. As they drew nearer they could see that the rear of the building had private docks on the riverfront.

Though cleaned up, the building's exterior still sported some features from its factory days, including decorative molding and wrought iron fire escapes that snaked down each side of the building. The grounds around the complex were beautifully maintained, every tree and blade of grass in its proper place. The afternoon sun reflecting off the nearby river painted the building in gold and silver light.

Joe whistled softly. "I bet this place sets Royal back a pretty penny every month." Frank nodded in agreement.

"Royal lives on the second floor," Chelsea said. "We can go up because there's no doorman during the day. But how are we going to get in?"

Joe ran a hand through his blond hair and smiled roguishly. "We're pretty clever about that," he said.

The three of them went through the lobby and

11

climbed a stairway that curved gracefully up to the second floor. The stairs emptied out onto a long narrow hallway. There was a door at each corner of the hall.

"Royal's condo is the one on the far left," Chelsea said, indicating one of the doors on the riverfront side. "He's got an amazing view of the river."

As the trio approached the door, Joe stopped abruptly and put a finger to his lips, hushing the others. "It sounds as if someone's inside," he whispered.

"Maybe he's come back!" Chelsea said. "I didn't see his car in the lot, but . . ." She approached the door and knocked tentatively. "Mr. Royal? Steven? It's me, Chelsea Sirkin." The sounds stopped; no one came to the door.

Frank's eyes narrowed. Something didn't seem right. "Let Joe and me handle this," he said to Chelsea. He put a hand on the doorknob and turned it; the door wasn't locked.

Frank gently pushed the door open and poked his head inside. Joe peered over his brother's shoulder to get a look, too.

"Chelsea," Joe said, "is Royal a bad housekeeper?"

"Well," Chelsea started, "he's not the neatest person . . ."

"A *really* bad housekeeper?" continued Joe.

Chelsea stepped forward to see what Joe meant. A small gasp escaped her lips as she peeked inside.

The doorway opened directly into the living room of the condo. It was a huge room with a high ceiling and a row of sliding-glass doors that led onto a balcony that overlooked the river. Royal apparently used the room as a workplace, too; a computer sat atop an old desk near the far wall. The whole place looked as though a hurricane had hit it.

Papers lay scattered all over the floor. The drawers of the desk had been pulled out, emptied, and left open. Pictures hung crooked on the walls, as if someone had searched behind them. The cushions had been removed from the overstuffed sectional couch and left on the rug. Looking toward the adjoining dining-room/kitchen area, Joe could see that someone had searched the pantry, too.

"Chelsea, did the police search the condo when you called them?" Frank asked.

"I don't know," she replied. "They said they'd checked and had seen no sign of foul play."

"Then my guess is that whoever we heard in this room a minute ago ransacked the place," Frank said. He bent down and examined the lock on the outside door. "Looks like it's been picked by someone who doesn't really know what he's doing. Plenty of fresh scratches around the lock hole."

A subtle movement on the far end of the balcony caught Joe's attention. One of the sliding doors had been left slightly ajar. "Look," Joe cried, pointing to a figure on the balcony. "There he is!"

# 2 Royal Friends and Foes

The Hardys sprang into action, bolting across the room and pushing open the sliding door. When the man on the balcony turned and saw them, he jumped over the railing.

"He must have made it onto the fire escape," Joe said. "I'll follow. You try to stop him out front."

"Right!" Frank replied. He darted back through the apartment, almost knocking Chelsea over as he headed for the front door.

Joe was right—there was a fire escape about six feet below the balcony. By the time he leaped onto it, the culprit had reached the ground and was beginning to run toward the parking lot.

There was no way Frank would reach the guy

in time if he had a car nearby. Joe had only one thing to do. Climbing over the railing of the fire escape, he tried to pick a soft-looking spot on the manicured lawn below. Then he jumped.

The ground didn't turn out to be as soft as he'd hoped, and Joe had the wind knocked out of him. He hadn't broken anything, though. "Hey!" he called after the man he was chasing. The man looked back and stumbled a bit, but continued running.

Joe scrambled to his feet and resumed the chase. The man was angling for the far corner of the parking lot now, and Joe knew that would give Frank and him a chance. As Joe hit the asphalt parking lot, he spotted Frank coming out of the front door. The culprit hadn't seen Frank because he was making a beeline for the lone car parked on the far side of the lot.

The man reached the car, a white Toyota compact, and fumbled with his keys. Frank got there just as the man finally got the door unlocked. "Hold it!" said Frank, leaning on the car door so it couldn't be opened wide enough for the man to get in.

The man spun and raised his hands in a defensive gesture. Frank balled up his fist, ready to throw a punch if the guy made a false move. As Joe reached the car, the man said plaintively, "I give up! Don't hurt me!"

Joe almost laughed, but Frank remained stern. "Who are you? What were you doing in Royal's condo?"

The man relaxed a bit. "I . . . I could ask you the same thing," he said.

"Look, you," Joe said, taking a menacing step forward, "don't give us any trouble."

The man backed up and raised his hands again, even though it was obvious to both Hardys that he had no idea how to defend himself in a fight. He was only about five-foot-eight and had curly reddish hair and a rectangular-shaped face. He wore a gray hooded sweatshirt and pants.

"I'm Zeb Winters, a friend of Royal's," the man said. "I came by to see him."

Just at that moment Chelsea caught up with the brothers. She had a cell phone in her hand. "Should I call the police?" she asked.

"We're not sure yet," Joe said. "Do you know this guy?"

Chelsea looked surprised. "Why, yes I do. He's Zeb Winters."

"And he's a friend of Royal's?" Frank asked.

"Ha!" Chelsea laughed. "Bitter rival is more like it. He and Royal have been trying to one-up each other for years."

Winters crossed his arms over his chest and sneered. "And I've won that battle more times than I've lost."

"Okay, wise guy," said Joe. "Now tell us why you're really here."

"Why should I?" Winters said.

"Because somebody ransacked that apartment, and right now you're our number-one suspect," Frank said.

"Hey," Winters complained, "Royal's place was tossed before I got there."

"We have only your word on that," Joe said. "If you didn't wreck the place, tell us why you came."

"Okay, okay. I came to confront Royal. I've seen his Town Called Chaos demo on the Internet, and I *know* that Royal stole my 3-D source code to make it. Town is way above Forest of Chaos, and Royal just doesn't have that much programming talent. Everybody in the industry knows that Anne Sakai was the brains behind that partnership. Royal's got a talent for marketing and promotion, yeah, and he's a pretty fair hacker, but there's no way he wrote that program himself."

"Who's Anne Sakai?" Frank asked.

Winters stared at Frank as though he couldn't believe the question. "Who is Anne Sakai?" Winters repeated. "She was just the woman who put Steven Royal on the map! She did the lion's share of programming on the first two Chaos games— everybody knows that."

"I remember that," Joe said. "Katherine Chaos was supposedly modeled on Sakai herself."

"Katherine Chaos was with Royal on the strategy book we saw, right?" Frank asked.

"She's the game's main character," Joe replied. "She's an adventurer like Indiana Jones, and a real looker, too. That's one of the reasons the Chaos games have been so popular."

"Yes, and that was Sakai herself in the picture with Royal."

"Wow," Joe said. "So the character *was* based on her."

"Okay," Frank said. "Where is this Sakai? If she and Royal broke off their partnership, we may want to talk to her, too."

Winters laughed. Chelsea said sheepishly, "You can't talk to her. She died in a plane crash two years ago."

"Yeah," Winters added. "Sharks got her body. Pretty nasty. She kicked off right after Caverns of Chaos. Royal had to do Forest of Chaos solo, which is why it stank. And that's why I know that Royal stole my source code. He *had* to because Sakai isn't around to help him with the programming."

"And I suppose you found proof of this in his apartment," Joe said sarcastically.

"Well, no," Winters admitted. "Like I said, I went up to confront Royal, but no one was home. His door was unlocked, though, so I went inside. I saw the place had been tossed, so I decided to look around on my own. Then you guys showed up. Who are you anyway?"

"We're working with Viking Software," Joe said. "We're looking for—"

Frank cut him off. "We're looking for someone who's been making threats against Royal and the company. And I'd say that you fit the profile."

"Look," Winters said, "I'm telling you that I didn't toss Royal's place."

"Then why'd you run?" Joe asked.

"I thought maybe *you* were the ones who wrecked the joint, and maybe you'd come back for another go. I wasn't about to stick around to find out."

"Well, I think you should stick around until the police check out your story," Joe said. He pulled Winters's car keys out of the door lock and pocketed them.

"Aw, come on!" pleaded Winters.

"Just sit tight. The cops'll be here in no time," Frank said. He nodded to Chelsea, and she punched the number into her cell phone. The Hardys turned to go back toward the condo.

"Hey!" Winters called after them. "Where are you guys going?"

"To make sure you didn't take anything from the apartment," Joe said, trying not to smile.

❖   ❖   ❖

When they got back to Royal's condo, Joe said, "Thanks for the save back there, Frank. I almost spilled to that guy that Royal is missing."

"Yeah," Frank said. "The fewer people who know, the better."

Chelsea caught up to them. "The police said they'd be here shortly."

"Then we'd better not waste any time," Frank said. "I doubt they'll let us search the place once they get here. Let's fan out. Joe, you take the back rooms, I'll take the front. Chelsea, see what you can find on Royal's computer. Try not to disturb any more evidence than we already have."

Chelsea and Joe nodded and the three set about their respective tasks. A few minutes later they gathered by the desk where Chelsea was working at the computer. Frank and Joe pulled up chairs and sat on either side of Phil's cousin.

"Only thing I found," Joe said, "is this letter." He held out a framed letter so the others could see it. "It's from someone named Ian Tochi. He says he's going to make trouble for Royal because of something in Forest of Chaos, though he doesn't say what."

"I know what that is," Chelsea said. "Tochi was an old friend of Royal's. He invented the Bombo Bear animatronic doll."

21

"You mean that sappy talking bear that spouted clichés about loving everybody?" Joe asked.

"What's so funny about peace, love, and understanding?" said Frank.

"That's the one," Chelsea said. "Anyway, Tochi got it in his head that the bear character in Forest of Chaos was a parody of Bombo. He's been making a stink about it ever since, but Royal never took it seriously."

"Seriously enough to have it framed," Frank said.

"That was just Steven's idea of a joke," Chelsea said. "I think he likes ticking people off."

"Which, I suppose, is why we're all here," Joe said. "You find anything, Frank?"

Frank shook his head. Just then the phone rang. Royal's answering machine picked it up after one ring. "This is Royal," the machine said in the game designer's voice. "I'm either off saving the world or conquering it. Leave a message."

"Not a big ego," Joe said sarcastically.

"Wait! Listen!" hissed Frank.

After the beep, the party on the other end of the line said, "This is Rosenberg. I'm waiting for you at my office, as you asked. But ten minutes from now, I won't be waiting any longer."

"He must be waiting for Royal," Joe said.

"Royal's sold us out!" Chelsea cried.

# 3 In Cahoots

Frank and Joe got to their feet at the same time. "If we're lucky," Frank said, "we can catch Royal and Rosenberg together."

"How do we get to Rosenberg's office?" Joe asked Chelsea.

Chelsea stammered out quick directions, and the Hardys headed for the door.

"You stay here and wait for the police," Frank told Chelsea. "We'll catch up with you after we talk to Rosenberg—and Royal."

Joe tossed Winters's keys to Chelsea on the way out. He and Frank made their way from the building to their van. A glance from Joe as they passed told Winters that he'd better stay put. The rival designer leaned his chin on his fists and fumed.

Driving quickly but carefully, Frank and Joe arrived at the offices of Wondersoft nine minutes later. It was a five-story building that looked as though it had been constructed in the nineteen twenties. Like most of the buildings in Jewel Ridge, it showed signs of recent renovation. A tastefully painted sign on the glass of the front door read, Wondersoft. The Hardys dashed inside and past the guard at the door.

"Mr. Rosenberg's expecting us," Frank said.

"We're here on behalf of Steven Royal," Joe added.

The guard nodded them past, and the Hardys made their way to the elevator bank at the center of the lobby. A sign there told them Rosenberg's office was on the top floor. They called the elevator and rode it up.

When they got off, they found themselves in a reception area, but the desk was deserted. Through an open door beyond the desk, they saw a balding, middle-aged man talking on the phone and smoking a cigar. He took the phone from his ear and stared at the brothers as they entered the room.

"Mr. Rosenberg?" Joe said, addressing the man. "I'm Joe Hardy, and this is my brother, Frank. We're here to talk to you about Steven Royal."

24

Rosenberg put down the phone. "The guard said you were on the way up. Where's Royal? He was supposed to be here an hour ago. Why didn't he come?"

"We were hoping you could tell us," Frank said. "We expected to meet him here with you."

Rosenberg took a pull on his cigar. "That Royal is a pain. If he weren't a genius, I'd never put up with him."

"So, you *have* seen him," Joe said.

"Not recently. I just got an e-mail from him this morning . . . Say, if you guys are with him, you should know that."

"We never said we were with him," Frank said. "We just said we were here to talk to you about him."

Rosenberg stood up behind his oak desk. "Who are you guys?" he demanded.

"We told you our names," Joe replied. "But if you're asking us what we're doing here, we're waiting for Steven Royal, same as you."

"We're investigators, working on a problem Royal's having with his present employer," Frank said.

"Police?" Rosenberg said, cocking the cigar to the side of his mouth.

"Private investigators," Joe said.

Rosenberg sat back down in his padded leather

chair and blew smoke. "Then I don't have to talk to you, do I?"

"That depends on who you'd rather talk to — the police or us," Frank said. "I'm sure the boys in blue will be happy to stop by here once they finish up at Royal's condo."

Rosenberg leaned forward and frowned. "What are the police doing at Royal's place?"

"Oh, sorry. We must have forgotten to tell you," Joe said, "Somebody broke into Royal's place and tossed his stuff. And since Royal's out of town, and since you were the last person to hear from him, I'm sure the police will want to talk to you."

"Okay, look," Rosenberg said, "I don't know anything about any break-in. All I know is I got an e-mail from Royal this morning, saying maybe he'd consider coming back to Wondersoft—if I made him the right offer. But, like I said, he never showed up. How was I to know he was out of town? Maybe the e-mail wasn't really from him. People are using the Internet to play pranks all the time."

"Could be," Frank said. "Maybe we could figure it out if you showed the note to us."

"Why should I do that?" Rosenberg asked, sounding suspicious.

"Because we want to help Royal out, just like you," Joe said. "And if we do, you might benefit."

Rosenberg pulled a piece of paper out of his

desk drawer. "You boys make a good team," he said, handing the paper to Frank.

Frank scanned the paper. "Mind if we keep this?" he asked.

"Go ahead," Rosenberg said. "I can always print another."

Frank nodded, then said to Joe, "We'd better check in with the police."

"Right," Joe said. "Here's our number in case you need to reach us." He scribbled the phone number of the van on a piece of paper and handed it to Rosenberg.

Rosenberg stood as the Hardys left his office. "Tell the cops I was helpful," he called after the brothers. "I don't want any trouble."

When they reached the van, Frank took the wheel and handed the paper to Joe. "See what you make of the note at the bottom," he said.

"Another riddle!" Joe said.

*The King is in the counting house; the Queen is in the dungeon. Their fortunes may be reversed when all the roosting bats come home. Side you with Ignorance or Knowledge? Seek not the apprentice, but the master.*

"This certainly seems to imply that Royal is in the money," Joe said. "But who is the Queen in the dungeon? Chelsea? She certainly is in hot water."

"Maybe," Frank agreed. "If she found Royal—and/or the game prototype—her fortunes would certainly be reversed. There's so much we don't know about this case yet. I hope Chelsea can shed more light on it."

Joe nodded, then said, "The return address on both the messages Royal sent are different, but I'm betting they came from the same machine. Do you think Phil could trace them?"

Frank smiled. "You bet he could. Call him and put him on it. I'm sure he'll take the time to help his cousin, even though he's working."

Joe called Phil Cohen on their car phone and gave him the info he needed. As they talked, Frank picked up some burgers and drinks from a drive-through. When they arrived back at the condo, the sun was setting and Winters's car was gone. They didn't see any signs of the police, either. They found Chelsea sitting on a picnic bench by the parking lot; she looked tired.

"The cops wouldn't let me stay in the condo," she said. "But I wasn't sure where you guys would end up, so I just hung out here."

"Too bad they kicked you out," Joe said. "I was hoping to poke around Royal's place a bit more."

"I did some more snooping while you were gone," Chelsea said. "But I didn't turn up anything useful."

"We brought you some food," Frank said, handing Chelsea a bag with a burger and drink. "We also put in a call to Phil, to see if he could trace your e-mail and another one that was sent to Rosenberg."

"Great. Thanks," she said, managing a weak smile. "I'm beat. Why don't we head back to my place and eat there. You can fill me in on what you found."

"Good idea," said Joe.

They all piled into the van and headed to Chelsea's apartment, which wasn't far away. Her home was both newer and smaller than Royal's, and it didn't have a view of the river.

The three of them finished eating, and then the Hardys filled Chelsea in on what they'd found out. Afterward she told them what had happened at the condo after they'd rushed off to see Rosenberg.

"Basically, the cops questioned Winters and me," she said. "He stuck to the story he'd told us— except when he told it to the police, he left out his being inside the condo. I just told the police the truth. Since they knew I'd been worried about Royal, they pretty much took me at my word. They looked over the condo, but didn't find anything."

"You mean, aside from the mess," Joe said.

"Yeah. They said the place had probably been robbed by someone who knew Royal was on vacation."

Joe nodded. "We gave Rosenberg a similar story," he said. "It makes a certain amount of sense."

"Only if you can believe the robber just happened to miss an expensive computer sitting in plain sight," Frank said.

Chelsea smiled. "Yeah. Jewel Ridge must have dumb crooks. Anyway, the cops kicked us out and sealed up the place—until Royal gets back, of course. They let Winters go because they really didn't have anything to hold him on. None of us even saw him in the condo. They promised to keep an eye on him, though, and also said they might want to talk to you guys. Check in with them before you leave."

"We're used to checking in with the police," Joe said.

"Okay," Frank said, "it looks as if Royal may have put one over on Rosenberg, too. Rosenberg wouldn't have called Royal here if he knew where Royal is. In fact, he seemed surprised when Joe and I hinted that Royal was out of town. Winters doesn't know Royal's gone, either. That sure doesn't leave us much to go on."

"Except for the riddles," Joe said. "I've been

thinking about them. If 'My past is the key to the future,' maybe we need to know more about Royal's past. What can you tell us, Chelsea?"

"Well," she began, "I did some research when we were trying to lure him to Viking Software. His is one of those typical came-out-of-nowhere computer genius stories. Apparently, he and Anne Sakai became friends in college—they had a mutual interest in computers and adventure gaming. Together they came up with Katherine Chaos and the Chaos saga idea. In their spare time, they programmed Caverns of Chaos. It sold well and they landed a contract with Wondersoft, but their second game, School of Chaos, really took off."

Chelsea took a sip of her drink and continued. "The two of them became famous in the computer gaming community. They traveled all over the world doing gaming conventions and promotional appearances. It probably helped that Anne looked a lot like the game's heroine.

"But in the end I guess that was a double-edged sword. Anne got a lot more attention than she wanted. Maybe she was really a loner at heart. So she cut out on the tour and went on vacation in the Caribbean. Unfortunately, she never came back. Her private plane crashed at sea and she died."

"Wow. What rotten luck," Joe said.

"Yeah," Chelsea said. "She was at the top of her profession before her death. I guess Royal took it pretty hard. But he did do another game, Forest of Chaos, without her. Unfortunately, it didn't do as well as the first two."

"For which Royal blamed Rosenberg," Frank added.

"Right, but the game really wasn't as good. With the new game, Royal seems to be back on track," Chelsea said. "A Town Called Chaos is a great game."

"What about what Winters said," Frank asked, "that Anne was the brains behind the games?"

"Well, if that were true, you couldn't tell it from the new game. It's way better than the first three. Personally, I think Sakai's death shook Royal, that's why the third game didn't turn out as well. Winters is just a jealous crank. A *talented* crank, but a crank nonetheless."

"Did Sakai have any relatives who could still be involved with the game?" Joe asked.

Chelsea wrinkled her forehead and thought a moment. "I'm not sure. I think she had heirs, but Royal never mentioned them. If you like, I can check at the office tomorrow. Do you think they might know where Royal is?"

"They could," Frank said. "And what about this Tochi character? Do you think he might have something to do with Royal's disappear-ance?"

"You mean, he might not have gone off on his own?" asked Chelsea, surprised.

"Yes," Frank said. "It's entirely possible that Steven Royal has been kidnapped."

# 4 Kidnapped?

"But you can't be serious," said Chelsea. "Who would want to kidnap Royal?"

"Could be someone out to get back at him, or at a rival company, or just someone who wants money," Frank said.

Chelsea looked puzzled. "But if they wanted money, why the riddles?"

Frank shrugged. "Possibly to throw us off. I'm not saying that Royal *has* been kidnapped. I'm just saying that we don't really have enough facts at this point to rule anything out. Steven Royal is missing; that's all we really know."

"So you think maybe Tochi kidnapped him?" Chelsea asked.

"At this moment anything is possible," Joe said.

"And Tochi did send that threatening letter that Royal had framed."

"It's just too much to think about tonight," Chelsea said. "I need some rest. We can start fresh in the morning."

"Good idea," Frank said. "Joe and I should be getting back to Bayport. It's a two-hour drive." He and Joe stood up to leave.

"I've got a spare sofa if you'd like to stay the night," Chelsea suggested.

"Well, it would save time . . ." Joe said.

"And we've got some extra clothes in the van," added Frank. "So, Ms. Sirkin, I guess you've got yourself a couple of houseguests."

"I'll call home and let them know what's up," Joe said.

"Check in with Phil, too," Frank suggested. "Maybe he's turned up something. I'll get some stuff out of the van."

Joe nodded. "Good idea."

Frank and Joe got up early and puzzled over the case as they made breakfast. Phil hadn't had anything to report.

When Chelsea finally joined them, she looked worn out. The Hardys could tell she hadn't slept well.

"What's the good word?" Chelsea asked sleepily.

"Waffles," Joe said. "Want some?"

35

She nodded and then took a seat at the small table in her combination kitchen/dining room. Joe plopped a plate of waffles in front of her and Frank poured the syrup and a glass of milk.

"Thanks, guys. I needed this," she said, taking a big forkful. A few bites later, she added, "You know, I've been thinking about Tochi. I think I read that he went to college with Royal and Sakai."

"So, all three of them shared a past," said Joe. "And now one is dead and another is missing."

At that moment the phone rang. Chelsea picked it up. After listening for a few seconds she handed the phone to Frank. "It's Phil."

Frank took the phone. "Hi, Phil. Found anything for us yet?" He nodded his head as Phil spoke. Joe edged closer to try to hear the conversation but couldn't pick up anything.

"Okay, that's great," Frank said. "Thanks. We'll get in touch if we need you again. No. Everything's fine here. Yeah. Goodbye." He hung up the phone.

"Well?" Joe asked, curious.

"Phil says that whoever sent the e-mails bounced them through a number of servers before they got to Viking and Wondersoft. That's why it took him so long to track them down."

"You mean like hiring a guy, who hires another guy, who hires a third guy to deliver a package so someone won't know it came from you," Joe said.

"Yeah. That's the general idea. The trick is finding that first guy." Frank smiled. "We're lucky that Phil knows what he's doing. Anyway, when he finished the trace, both e-mails originated at the same place: the mainframe computer at Northern Connecticut University."

"Northern Connecticut University?" Chelsea said. "That's where Sakai, Royal, and Tochi went to school!"

"Hey," Frank said, "that makes sense with the last riddle. Remember that bit about 'ignorance or knowledge,' and 'seek . . . the master?' Well, colleges turn ignorance into knowledge, and 'master' could be another word for teacher."

"And 'apprentice' for student," Joe added.

"Which all ties in to the clue about the past—Royal's past—being the future," Chelsea said, smiling just a bit.

"It looks like we're going to have to take a tour of Royal's personal history to find your game prototype, Chelsea," Frank said.

"Then I'd say that Northern Connecticut University is our next stop," concluded Joe.

"Coming with?" Frank asked Chelsea.

"I think I should stay here and coordinate

things from the office. Plus, Dave will want to know what you guys have dug up. Don't forget to check in with the police."

"We'll talk to them on the way out of town," Joe said.

Chatting with the police took longer than Frank and Joe expected. Unfortunately, the conversation didn't give the Hardys any new leads. It was late morning when Frank and Joe finally began the trip from Jewel Ridge to Chisholm, Connecticut, where the university was located. Because of highway construction, it took almost three hours to get there.

At the library, Frank and Joe posed as students doing a summer advanced-placement research paper and obtained permission to use the library. The librarian checked their Bayport High IDs and gave them a temporary password in order to use the computer for the day.

Summer had emptied the college of most students, and Frank and Joe had little trouble finding a free terminal. They called Phil, who told them how to get past the computer's security systems so they could get into the files they needed.

"Here are Royal's academic records," Joe said. "But I don't really see anything that'd lead us to him. Looks like he was a pretty average student.

Didn't cause any trouble. Paid his bills on time. Not much else."

"Cross-reference him with the school newspaper database," Frank suggested.

"Okay. There's more here. Some stuff about him and Sakai creating their own game. An article about the Chaos series. An award he, Sakai, and Tochi won for being entrepreneurs. Things about Tochi, too. An article about Bombo Bear. Hey!"

"What?"

"Looks like Tochi's still here," Joe said. "He's working as an assistant professor of engineering."

Frank nodded. "That's interesting. Since he works here, he has easy access to the computer system every day. See if there's anything else, and then we'll look him up before we leave town."

"I could probably get his address from the database and . . . What?"

Frank leaned over his brother's shoulder so he could see the computer screen better. "What is it? What's wrong?"

"Something funny just happened to the computer," Joe said. "It froze up—crashed or something." He typed a few commands, but nothing happened. Then, suddenly, the screen came back to life. A message appeared.

*Riddles in the ether, riddles in the tunnels.*
*Past and future, you decide. Caught between*

*History and Art. Oh, what a tangled web we weave!*

The message flashed a few times and then disappeared. Fortunately, Joe had scribbled it down.

"Looks like the games aren't over," Frank said.

"What I want to know," Joe said, "is how this guy knows where we are."

"He probably doesn't," said Frank. "He's good with computers, so he could have created a program to keep watch on his files. Anyone checking them would cause the message to pop up."

"And we just happened to be the lucky victims," Joe said. "Makes sense. Now let's see if we can make sense of this riddle."

"Okay, if this riddle—the one that just appeared and vanished—is the riddle in the ether, then the next clue must be the riddles in the tunnel," Frank said. "Then more stuff about the past and future. . . . Hmm."

"In School of Chaos, there were some steam tunnels with treasure in them," Joe said. "Hey! Don't some college campuses use steam tunnels for heating? Let me check something. . . ." Joe typed a few commands into the computer and found the article he wanted.

"Frank, check this out," he said. "In the article about the Chaos series, it says that the School of Chaos is loosely based on the NCU campus."

"Bring up a heating plan of the university," Frank said. "See if there are any steam tunnels here."

"Way ahead of you," Joe said, already typing commands into the computer. Moments later a diagram of the tunnels popped up on the screen. "Wow. Looks like a giant spiderweb."

Frank smiled. "Fits right in with the riddle, doesn't it? Now, how do we figure out where to look in the tunnels? Searching the whole system could take days."

"I bet there's another clue in the riddle," Joe said. "What about this . . . 'Caught between Art and History.' Maybe that isn't just another reference to his past."

"You're right, Joe! It could refer to a place on campus. So the next clue could be in the tunnels between the art and history buildings. What are we waiting for? Let's go."

"Can we grab something from a vending machine on the way?" said Joe. "I'm famished!"

"Okay," Frank said. "We'll pick up our backpacks from the car, too. We might need supplies. Who knows what's down in those tunnels?"

"In the game there was treasure," Joe said.

"What, no monsters?" Frank asked.

"Well, now that you mention it . . . I guess there were monsters, too."

Stopping at the van and finding food didn't

slow the Hardys down much. Nor did the lock on the door to the tunnels under the history building. Joe opened it with his lock pick in just seconds. The door creaked ominously as they swung it open and peered into the dark tunnel beyond. Joe reached for the light switch and flicked it on. Nothing happened.

"Must have burned out," he said.

Frank pulled a flashlight from his backpack. "Be prepared," he said.

"Frank, you are such a Boy Scout," Joe said, and laughed as he pulled out his flashlight, too. Joe led the way down the tunnel.

Huge steam pipes ran along the walls and ceiling of the tunnel, leaving a clear path down the middle for a person to walk. "Doesn't look like anybody's been down here in a while," Joe said. He brushed his fingers along the insulation of one pipe, and they came up dusty.

"That would explain the lights," Frank said. "But be careful, just in case."

"Yeah, watch yourself. There's water on the floor."

"Boy," Frank said sarcastically, "that'd be unusual in a steam tunnel."

Joe laughed and kept walking. "At least there are no monsters."

"Joe, look out!"

Frank rushed forward, but he was too late. Joe

had already tripped on a thin strand of wire strung across the corridor a few inches above the floor. Frank grabbed Joe's shirt to try to keep him from falling, but Joe's momentum pulled his brother down with him.

Instead of hitting the cement floor of the tunnel, Joe and Frank landed on soft netting.

"Boy," Joe said, "lucky this net was here."

"Maybe not so lucky," Frank replied. "I'm stuck."

"Hey, me, too!" Joe said. Sure enough, the sticky strands of the netting held them tight.

"Joe, this isn't a net," Frank said. "It's a giant spiderweb!"

# 5  The Spider

"Joe," Frank said, "in the School of Chaos game, are the monsters in the steam tunnels *spiders?*"

"Now that you mention it, yeah, they are. Good thing this is real life, and not a video game."

"Right at the moment, Joe, I'm not so sure. Look!" Frank raised his arm and pointed.

Joe glanced up at the steam pipes running above their heads. Something was scurrying along the pipes. Joe pointed his flashlight at it, and then immediately wished he hadn't. A giant black and yellow spider skittered along a pipe toward the brothers.

"Shoo! Shoo! Go away!" Joe said. The creature seemed to be the size of a salad plate and had red eyes.

"I didn't know spiders grew that big," Frank said.

"No, neither did I, but obviously this one has mutated down here," Joe answered, trying to make sense of the size of the spider.

As Joe and Frank pulled webbing off themselves, more of the sticky mesh adhered. "I don't like this game anymore. Could you log us off and shut down the computer, please, Frank?" Joe said.

"Wish I could, Joe."

Just then the spider began to descend toward the brothers on a long strand of silk spun from its abdomen.

"I can't reach my backpack," Frank said, struggling against the sticky strands. "Can you reach yours?"

"No. But . . . wait a minute, I might be able to reach my front pocket. Slow that spider down, will you, Frank?"

"I'll try." Frank still had his flashlight in his hand. He took careful aim with it, using all the skills he'd acquired as a pitcher in baseball. When he knew he had the distance, Frank flung the flashlight at the spider as hard as he could.

It hit the arachnid, but didn't knock it from its web. Instead, it set the spider swinging. The creature flailed wildly, trying to regain its balance. It made a strange clicking sound as it struggled.

"Nice job, Frank," Joe said, and pulled out his pocketknife, which he deftly opened with one hand.

He cut through the strands of webbing that had his upper body trapped. By that time, though, the spider had stopped its silk line from swinging and was beginning its deadly descent toward the brothers once more.

"Oh no, you don't!" said Joe. He stripped off his backpack and swung it with all his might at the spider, now only a few feet away. The pack connected and the spider went flying.

The creature smashed against the tunnel wall with a crunch. Then it fell to the floor. A few seconds later it stopped moving.

"Great work, Joe!" yelled Frank.

"Best hit I've had all year," said the younger Hardy. It didn't take him long to free Frank from the web also.

"That was close," Joe added.

"Maybe not as close as we thought," Frank said. He moved toward the fallen spider. "This spider isn't real."

"I knew there was something wrong with it." Shining his flashlight on the thing's body, Joe could see that it had broken open. The creature's insides were made up of wires, gears, and electronic circuitry. "I don't know whether to be glad it's not real, or frightened. Royal went to a lot of trouble to scare us with this one."

Frank had retrieved his flashlight and taken out his pocketknife. He began poking around the innards of the spider. "Sure did. It doesn't seem to be booby-trapped. . . . What's this?" He stuck his fingers into the machine and pulled out a thin, metallic sheet.

"Looks like foil paper," Joe said.

"That's exactly what it is," Frank said as he unfolded the sheet. A message was written on the papery inner surface.

*The Forest is not my work, but you'll find my work there. Seek the primeval cave, for the golden prize lies within. The past and future are at hand!*

"Boy, am I getting tired of these riddles," Joe said. "And all this past-future stuff."

"This sounds like it might be the end of the game. So, what do you make of it?"

"Well, Chelsea said that Tochi claimed Royal had put a parody of Bombo Bear in Forest of Chaos. That's why Tochi sent that threatening note," Joe said.

Frank nodded. "Which would explain the 'work' reference—if Tochi wrote this. But what about the primeval cave?"

"I don't know," Joe said. "But I'm betting that Chelsea would know. And Tochi might, too. Do you think that he and Royal could have stopped feuding? Could they be working together on this prank?"

"If they are, I don't much like their senses of humor."

Joe frowned. "Neither do I."

Frank scooped up the mechanical spider and put it in his backpack. "Let's go have a talk with Professor Tochi."

After checking the rest of the tunnel for more clues, or traps, the Hardys went back to their van. On the way, they stopped at a phone booth and got Tochi's address. He lived just off campus. The sun had set by the time the Hardys hit the road again.

As they were driving to Tochi's place, their car phone rang. Joe was behind the wheel, so Frank picked it up.

"I'm glad I caught you guys," Phil Cohen's voice said. "I'm afraid I gave you a bum steer."

Frank punched the speaker function so that Joe could hear the call, too. "How do you mean, Phil?" Frank asked.

"It looks like whoever sent those messages is more clever than I thought. The university is just being used as a clearinghouse for the notes. They really came from someplace in Europe."

"Well, that's strange," Joe said. "We're pretty convinced that someone right here in town is mixed up in this."

"That might make it easier to access the computer to use it as a front," Phil said. "And this European lead could be another red herring. I'll have to look into it further."

"Have you heard from Chelsea?" Frank asked.

"Yeah," Phil said. "Her whole office is still in an uproar, and I can't blame them."

"We'll call her after we follow up on this lead," Joe said.

"Good idea," said Phil. "I'll keep in touch. Call if you need me." He hung up.

Frank switched off the speaker. "You ever feel like Alice in Wonderland?" he asked Joe.

"Curiouser and curiouser," said Joe, smiling. "Let's find Tochi."

Three minutes later they pulled up in front of Tochi's house. It was a small, two-story Victorian with a large porch running around the front and one side. It hadn't been maintained well, even though the grass had been mowed recently. Frank figured that Tochi didn't have the time, temperament, or salary needed to keep the place up. He wondered how much money an assistant professor made—probably not nearly as much as a successful game designer like Royal, he guessed.

Though it had grown dark, Frank and Joe saw no lights on inside the house.

"Think he's home?" asked Frank.

Joe shrugged and got out of the car. "Let's find out." Frank followed. The brothers strolled up onto the porch and knocked on the front door. No one answered. Frank moved to a nearby window and peered inside.

"I don't see anyone," he said. "But it's pitch black inside."

"Get out your flashlight," Joe said. "I'll try the door." He did—the knob turned and the door swung open. "What do you know, it must be our lucky day."

"Maybe," Frank said. He bent down and checked the lock with his flashlight. "Picked—badly. Just like Royal's. We'd better go in and look around. But be careful. This could be another trap."

Joe nodded and Frank switched on his flashlight. The brothers stepped inside the house and looked around. "Uh-oh," said Frank. "Looks like someone got here before we did."

"Again," added Joe. "Just like at Royal's."

The room was a mess, couch undone, pictures crooked, papers on the floor.

"Do you think Winters could have done this?" Joe asked.

"Could be," Frank said. "The police didn't hold

him. See if you can find a light. We'd better make sure that no one is hurt in here."

"Check."

Before Joe could move, though, a menacing voice from behind stopped both Hardys dead in their tracks.

"Hold it!" the voice said. "Move one inch and you're toast!"

# 6 Big Bad Bear

"Should we put our hands up, or down?" Joe asked.

"Don't do anything," the voice said. "I'm going to turn on the lights. And I swear, if you move, I'll fry you."

"Must be some deranged short-order cook," Joe whispered to Frank.

"I heard that. And I'm not kidding," the voice said. "You guys are in big trouble." The lights came on. The room looked even worse in the light. "What have you done to my house?" cried the voice.

Frank and Joe stole looks over their shoulders. In the doorway stood a man of medium height and stocky build. He had curly hair and a thick black mustache. He didn't look too much older than the Hardys. In his hand he held a small black box with a pistol grip. Frank and Joe recognized it as a stun gun.

"Are you Ian Tochi?" Frank asked. "We came to see you," said Joe.

"So you could do what, wreck my place?" Tochi said. He sounded both nervous and angry.

"We didn't do this," Frank said. "But we thought someone might be hurt in here—that's why we came in."

"A likely story," Tochi said.

"Look, if you want to check our credentials, call Officer Con Riley at the Bayport PD," Joe said. "We've worked with him before. Tell him Joe and Frank Hardy said you should call. His number is . . ."

"I can look up his number," Tochi said. "You could just be giving me the number of a confederate." Tochi edged over to a nearby phone, fumbled with the receiver, and called the operator. A few minutes later he'd talked to Riley. He had the police officer describe the Hardys, and seemed relieved and a bit less nervous as he hung up the phone.

"Okay," Tochi said. "You match the descriptions that cop gave me, but I'd like to see your ID anyway. You, the tall, dark-haired one. Take your ID out slowly and show it to me."

Frank did as Tochi asked. When he was done, Tochi put down the stun gun. "Sorry about that," he said. "But it's not every day you come home to find your house ransacked and a couple of guys prowling around. What do you want, anyway?"

"We wanted to find out what you know about Steven Royal," Frank said. "Have you seen him lately?"

"Ha!" Tochi said. "As if I'd want to. That guy is a jerk! Why did you want to ask me about him?"

"We're trying to talk to all his old friends," Joe said. "He's playing games with his new publisher, running them around on a wild-goose chase."

"Sounds like Steve. But I haven't seen him since the last time we were in court."

"You mean about Bombo Bear?" Frank asked.

Tochi looked surprised. "You know about that? Of course, the suit didn't go anywhere, and I didn't have the money to continue pursuing it."

"I thought you made a pile off Bombo," Joe said.

"You'd be surprised how fast the money goes," Tochi said, smiling sheepishly. "Especially when you're in college. And I didn't have the best agreement with the toy manufacturer, either. Now, the sales on Bombo are practically nonexistent. Luckily, I finished going to school so I could get this assistant professor position. A lot of inventors deliver mail for a living. At least I get to teach mechanical engineering."

He sighed. "Things would have been a lot different, though, if Anne Sakai and I had hooked up on that computer game as we planned."

"I thought she was Royal's partner," Frank said.

"Partner isn't exactly the right word for it," Tochi said. "She put up with him. That's all anyone ever does. Sure, they worked well together, but it's not like they were married or anything. Royal was good at all the things she hated, like publicity and personal appearances. The two of them fought like cats and dogs most of the time. If he'd been around when her plane crashed, I'd have guessed he'd killed her."

"Do you think someone killed her, then?" Joe asked.

"Oh, no. It was just a freak accident. Anne was good with planes. She had a real knack with anything mechanical."

"You must be pretty good with mechanical things yourself," Frank said. He gave Joe a glance that reminded the younger Hardy of the mechanical spider in Frank's backpack.

"That's why I got my teaching job," Tochi said. "I'm not like Anne, though. She had a real gift. If it was mechanical, she could fix it; if it was a computer she could program it. She'd have gotten her doctorate in no time if she hadn't become a computer gaming star. She even helped me build the original Bombo prototype. You know the way he moves his jaws when he talks? That was her idea."

Joe and Frank nodded.

Tochi sighed again. "If only Royal hadn't lured her into his video game racket. Yeah . . . she and I could have made a great Bombo computer game together. If she hadn't died, I could have had a real Bombo adventure out, instead of having to suffer Royal's parody in Forest of Chaos. I'm an idiot when it comes to computers."

Suddenly an idea occurred to Joe. "Is Royal good with machines like Sakai was? Did he help you with the Bombo prototype?"

"The answer to that is, no and no," said Tochi. "Royal is all thumbs. He couldn't find his nose in a dark room using both hands."

"One last question," Joe said. "Do you know what the primeval cave is? It was in one of Royal's riddles."

"*Primeval* means 'early' or 'original,' so maybe it means the first game—Caverns of Chaos."

Joe nodded.

"Well, I guess that gives us everything we need to know," Frank said. He motioned to Joe that they should head for the door.

"No problem," Tochi said. "At least now I know you're not burglars. Guess I should call the police."

"You probably should, Mr. Tochi," Frank said. He paused at the door and looked back. "Tochi . . . that's Italian, isn't it?"

"On my dad's side," Tochi said.

"Spend any time in Italy?" Frank asked.

"Some," Tochi said. "Quite a bit when I was a kid. And I try to go back every couple of years. A lot of my family still lives there."

"Well, thanks again," Frank said. He and Joe walked to their van. "Let's head back to Jewel Ridge," Frank said. "I think we've gotten all the info we'll get here."

As they headed down the highway, Joe asked, "So, what was that bit checking Tochi's genealogy?"

"Remember when Phil said that he'd traced the computer messages to Europe?"

"You're thinking it's Italy, then?" Joe asked.

"Could be," Frank said. "We may have another piece of the puzzle."

"This puzzle has too many pieces if you ask me," Joe said. "According to the people we've talked to, Royal just doesn't have the know-how to pull this kind of stunt. Winters says Royal couldn't do the computer stuff; Tochi says Royal couldn't have made that mechanical spider."

"One of them could be helping Royal, of course," Frank said. "Or either one could be lying to us. Anne said Winters had the computer talent. Tochi sure has the mechanical ability."

57

"But both those guys really seem to hate Royal and probably wouldn't work with him," Joe said, leaning back in the passenger seat as Frank drove. "Rosenberg would love to have Royal free from his contract with Viking Software. But that still leaves the big question: Where is Royal?"

Frank nodded. "It's a tricky case, that's for sure. Maybe Chelsea can help us crack the clue we found in the spider. Or maybe the spider itself will give us some clue."

"I hope so," Joe said. "Let's call Chelsea and then get something to eat. I think better on a full stomach."

Chelsea was still at the office. No new information on Royal had come in, and her co-workers were getting even more worried. She said she had some work to finish, but would meet the Hardys at her apartment when they got back into town.

After that, Frank and Joe picked up some doughnuts and coffee, but the food didn't stimulate any new ideas. They were feeling pretty tired when they got back to Jewel Ridge three hours later.

Frank was pulling the van into Chelsea's parking lot just in time to see Chelsea walk along the well-lit path to the building from the lot.

She stopped just outside the main door of the apartment house as a white Toyota pulled up beside her. The passenger side door of the car opened and Chelsea stooped down to talk to someone the Hardys couldn't see. She looked angry. Then without warning a hand reached out, grabbed Chelsea's wrist, and started to drag her into the car.

# 7 Car Problems

Frank stepped on the gas and twisted the wheel. The tires of the van screeched as Frank shot around a row of cars and pulled in front of the white Toyota.

As Chelsea pulled back against the person trying to drag her into the car, Joe and Frank leapt out of the van.

"Let her go!" Joe shouted. He dashed over to Chelsea, while Frank circled over to the driver's side and yanked the car door open.

He cocked his fist back and said, "Do it! Now!"

The person in the car let go, and Joe caught Chelsea as she toppled backward.

Frank reached into the car with his free hand and pulled someone out. "Zeb Winters!" he said.

"I thought we might expect more trouble from you."

Zeb put his hands up as if to say "Who? Me?" But what came out of his mouth was, "The lady and I were just having a little conversation."

"That kind of conversation can get you arrested," Frank said. He still had his fist aimed at Zeb's face but hadn't decided whether or not to punch him.

Joe joined Frank on the driver's side of the car. "Or if not arrested, in big trouble with the lady's friends." If possible, Joe seemed even angrier than Frank. He looked ready to punch Zeb, too.

"Hey, all I wanted to do was talk to her," Winters said. "Sorry if I got a little rough."

"We'll get a little rough with *you* if you try anything like that again," Joe said. Frank let his arm drop; the moment for cleaning Winters's clock had passed.

Chelsea glared at Winters. "He's been annoying me all day," she said. "Following me around and making phone calls to the company."

"Like I said, I only wanted to talk to her," complained Winters. "Find out what she knows about Royal stealing my 3-D code."

"I told you," Chelsea said angrily, "Steven Royal did *not* steal your programming code for A Town Called Chaos."

"You don't know that for sure," Winters said

smugly. "Only Royal knows, and he's conveniently missing. But if you showed me the game demo, I could figure it out."

Chelsea crossed her arms over her chest and glared at him. "There is not one person in Viking Software stupid enough to let you see that program. No way are we going to let you do to us what you're accusing Steven of doing."

"That sounds pretty final to me," Joe said to Winters. "If I were you, I'd take that answer and go away. Run very fast and very far—away from here. Got it?"

"Any more stuff like this and you'll be talking to the cops . . . again," Frank added.

Winters grumbled and then zoomed off into the night.

"I'm really starting to dislike that guy," Frank said as he watched Winters go.

"Zeb Winters is a first-class jerk," added Chelsea. "If he weren't such a talented programmer he'd have been out of work long ago. Come on, let's go inside and have some coffee. You can tell me what you've dug up."

"Maybe we could call out for a pizza, too," suggested Joe.

"Good idea," Chelsea said. "I've been so frantic today, I didn't really eat much." All three of them went up to Chelsea's apartment.

Frank filled Chelsea in on what little they'd

found while Joe ordered the pizza. When he was done, Chelsea flopped onto her couch. "What a nightmare this day has been!" she said. "Not only did I have Winters harassing me, but Ron Rosenberg called Dave and claimed that our contract with Royal is invalid. He said Royal promised he'd come back to Wondersoft. Rosenberg's lawyers are supposed to stop by the office in the next day or two. Dave is completely freaked out."

"That sounds like an intimidation tactic to me," Frank said.

"Yeah," Joe called back from the kitchen. He'd taken it upon himself to make some coffee. "Unless Rosenberg's turned up something new since last night. He sure can't hang a case on that e-mail he got. We can't even be sure if it really came from Royal."

"Speaking of e-mail," Frank said, "we should check in with Phil to see if he's turned up anything new."

"Oh, I almost forgot in all the excitement," Chelsea said. "Phil called me just before I left. He said that his computers at home couldn't take the e-mail trace any further. He needed something more powerful. Dave and I offered him the computers at our office; they're state-of-the-art.

"Phil's going to drive up tomorrow morning. I'm glad he can help out because we just don't have the manpower to tackle this kind of thing right now. All our best computer people are jammed with work."

"It'll be good to have him here," Frank said. "We might need his expertise."

"And we're doing so well on our own," Joe said sarcastically as he brought in the coffee. "I was pretty sure that Zeb was behind the ransacking of Tochi's apartment—until you told us he'd been here all day. His bothering you and Viking continuously doesn't leave him any time to drive to NCU and back."

Frank nodded. "Yeah. Though that doesn't rule out Zeb, or anyone else, helping Royal on this crazy stunt. None of the suspects we've got seem to have the skills to pull this prank off by themselves. Not even Royal."

"But the only one who has a motive to help Royal in messing with Viking is Rosenberg," Joe said. "The other two guys seem to hate Royal's guts. Hey, do you think maybe this is some kind of a scheme by Royal and Rosenberg to break Royal's contract with Viking?"

"If it is," Frank said, "Rosenberg would need really great lawyers to pull it off. The courts would frown upon antics like this."

"Well, it doesn't seem much like a prank to me, or my company," Chelsea said. "This stunt could cost us everything."

"And maybe that's Royal and Rosenberg's plan.

If Viking went out of business, Royal's contract would be void, wouldn't it?" Joe asked.

"I'd have to ask our lawyers," Chelsea said. "I suspect that Dave is having them go over that contract with a fine-tooth comb right about now."

Just then the doorbell rang. "Pizza man," said a voice on the intercom.

Chelsea got up to press the button to buzz him in, then stopped. "I hope it's not Zeb again. I wouldn't put it past him to hang around and bribe the delivery guy."

Frank and Joe got up. "We'll go downstairs to get it," said Frank. He and Joe exited the apartment and went down to the front door.

When they got there they found a delivery boy waiting with their pizzas. Frank paid the bill and watched the kid walk back to his truck.

"Doesn't look old enough to drive, does he?" Joe said. "Hey! Who's that messing with the van?"

Sure enough, someone was prowling around the Hardys' van. The brothers set the pizzas down and dashed out the door for their car.

"If this is Winters again, I'm going to deck him for sure," Joe said.

"Not if I do it first," Frank said.

The figure poking around the van didn't notice the Hardys coming. Joe grabbed the person by the shoulder and said, "What do you think you're doing?"

The person spun around. She was a medium-tall, thin woman in a tan trench coat and slouch hat. She had short-cropped black hair and a roundish face. She wasn't much older than the Hardys, but her outfit—a fedora and trench coat—reminded Frank of something from a thirties detective movie.

"Me?" said the woman. She seemed shocked at being caught. Frank and Joe nodded solemnly at her. "I was just looking around. I'm buying a new car soon, and I was thinking about buying this kind of van."

"It looked like you were trying to *break into* this *particular* van," Joe said.

"No, no. You've misunderstood," the woman said.

"Maybe the police should decide if we've misunderstood," Frank said.

The woman sighed and her shoulders slouched forward a bit. "Okay, you got me. No need to call the police. My name is Samantha Rockford, my friends call me Sam. I'm a private detective working for Ron Rosenberg. Do you know him?"

"We've met," Joe said. Something about this woman didn't seem right to him. Perhaps it was her clothes, or maybe it was the way she kept glancing around as she spoke. She seemed to be looking for something, though Joe couldn't spot what.

"Well," Sam continued, "he hired me to check up on Steven Royal. Rosenberg says he's gone missing."

"Really?" Joe said, raising an eyebrow at his brother.

"And why are you *here?*" Frank asked.

"I was checking Royal's known associates. When I saw you guys fraternizing with Sirkin before, I figured you might know something about the case."

"So you decided to break into our van," Joe said. "Doesn't ring true to me, Frank."

"Me neither," said the elder Hardy. "Let's take her inside and let the police sort it out." He took Sam by the arm and urged her toward the apartment door.

"This really isn't necessary," Sam said. She tried to pull away, but Frank's grip held her gently in place.

As they walked toward the apartments, Chelsea poked her head out of the lobby door. She had the pizzas in her arms. "Hey, guys," she said. "What's going on?" Then her eyes went wide. "Look out!"

At the same moment Chelsea screamed, Frank and Joe heard the roar of a car engine behind them. They turned in time to see a blue sedan barreling down on them at full speed.

# 8 Crack Up

Frank pushed Sam one way, and he and Joe dove in the other direction. The speeding car whizzed between the two groups, missing them all.

Before it could change direction or brake, the car slammed into a concrete pylon at the bottom of one of the parking lot's light poles. The sedan's engine revved for a couple of seconds more, and then the engine died.

Frank and Joe got up and looked at the wreck. "Oh, man!" Joe said. "Whoever's inside there must be really messed up."

The brothers ran to the car to try to rescue the driver. Chelsea dashed over to join them. "Frank! Joe! Are you all right?"

"Better than whoever's in here," Joe said, trying

to open the crumpled driver's-side door. He tried to peer inside, but the front and side windows of the car had shattered into a million spiderwebs of glass.

All Joe could see was a large white blob in the driver's seat. He couldn't make out the driver's head, or even his arms, just an indistinct shape. He feared that the person inside had been crushed beyond recognition.

He let out a relieved sigh when he realized what had really happened. "The air bag deployed," Joe said. "But it's blocking my view. I can't see anything else."

"Neither can I," said Frank. He had been trying to look into the passenger side of the car. But that side had crumpled against the pylon. The wreckage prevented Frank from seeing inside. "Maybe the driver's still alive," he said, joining Joe on the driver's side of the car.

Chelsea looked at the car, then at the brothers. "This is Steven Royal's car," she said, a note of fear and sadness in her voice.

"What a way to end a case," Joe said. He pulled on the door handle, but the door didn't budge.

"Let me help," said Frank.

He and Joe positioned themselves so they could both get a good grip on the door handle.

"On three," Frank said. Joe nodded at him. Frank counted. "One . . . two . . . *three!*"

The brothers pulled hard on the door, and slowly it creaked open, metal scraping against metal. The air bag fell away from the seat as the door opened.

"Holy cats!" Joe said. "There's no one inside!"

Sure enough, the driver's seat was empty.

"Just like in A Town Called Chaos," Chelsea muttered.

"Cars can't drive themselves," Frank said, turning his scientific eye to the sedan's steering column. "There has to be some kind of remote-controlled steering device here."

"I'm sure there is," Joe said. "But maybe we'd better let the police poke around inside the car. They'll be here any minute."

Now that he was listening, Frank could hear police sirens; they weren't very far off. Someone in the apartments must have called them.

"Well, they won't be able to shrug this off," Frank said. "Whether it was Royal controlling this car or someone else, this stunt could have seriously hurt us."

"And Sam," Joe said. He looked around. "Say, where did she go? Chelsea, did you see where Sam Rockford went?"

"Is she the woman in the trench coat who was with you? I was so worried about you guys, I didn't pay any attention to her after you pushed her out of harm's way," Chelsea said. "Who was she?"

"A PI working for Rosenberg," Frank said. "Maybe."

"She seemed to know Royal was missing, though we didn't tell Rosenberg that," Joe added.

Chelsea sighed. "As if we didn't have enough trouble!"

The police took Royal's disappearance much more seriously now. They impounded the wreck of Royal's car and took it to the police lab for testing. They also spent a couple of hours talking to Frank, Joe, and Chelsea. During the course of the interrogation, the Hardys learned that the police's new theory was that Royal's disappearance was part of a publicity stunt.

They didn't seem to believe that Chelsea and Viking Software had been trying to keep Royal's absence secret. "After all," the lead detective told Chelsea, "you've been camped on our doorstep making a fuss for most of the last week. You've done your jobs as concerned citizens; now let us do our jobs. The only thing you should worry about at the moment is keeping your noses clean. If any of you are involved in this stunt, then you could all be in big trouble. Let the Jewel Ridge PD worry about Steven Royal. This car wreck proves he's lurking around here somewhere.

"And you, Hardy boys," the detective continued, "make sure you stay out of the way of our in-

71

vestigation. Maybe the police in Bayport need help from amateurs, but in Jewel Ridge, we do things by the book."

Frank and Joe silently decided not to turn the mechanical spider over to the cops, though they did mention the ransacking of Tochi's house. By the time the trio got back into Chelsea's apartment, the pizza they'd ordered had been cold a long time. They stuffed it into the fridge and went straight to bed.

They were awakened late the next morning by the repeated ringing of Chelsea's doorbell. Joe roused himself from the couch and answered the intercom. "Yeah," he said sleepily. "What is it?"

"It's me, Phil," said a voice on the other end of the intercom. "Buzz me in, will you?" Joe pressed the buzzer and a minute later Phil came through the door, looking well-rested and eager to begin working. Frank got out of the recliner and Chelsea joined them from the other room.

The four friends sat around Chelsea's dining room table and had granola and milk for breakfast. They brought Phil up to date on everything that had happened the last two days. The Hardys also pulled out the remains of the mechanical spider for Phil to see.

"Seems to me," Phil said between mouthfuls of cereal, "that you could buy most of the material in this spider at an electronics supply store.

Though some of it looks like it might have been scavenged from toys."

"Which could point to Tochi's involvement," Joe said.

Phil nodded as he ate. "Mm. Or someone with that amount of skill."

"Chelsea," Frank said, "what do you make of the clue we found inside the spider? I thought the forest reference meant the Forest of Chaos game and the caverns meant the Caverns of Chaos game. That would make sense since Caverns was the first game and *primeval* means 'original.' But I can't imagine that Royal hid clues to finding the prototype in those old games. No one thinks that far ahead."

"Could the forest and the cave be real places?" Joe asked. "And if they are, where are they?"

Chelsea's eyes lit up. "They *could* be," she said. "When I was reading up on Royal when Viking brought him on board, I read a lot of magazine articles on the origin of the Chaos series.

"Royal and Sakai used to go camping in Kendall State Park, in western Massachusetts. According to one article, the two of them got the idea for the original Caverns of Chaos game when they found a hidden cave somewhere in the park.

"The reporter couldn't find any record of such a cave, but he couldn't prove it didn't exist, either. Royal claimed that he and Sakai had hidden the cave entrance to keep out snoopers. He wouldn't say where it was. Even though nobody's found it since then, maybe it *is* a real place," Chelsea concluded.

"And if it is," Frank said, "then the prototype—the treasure—might be there. That's what the clue implies, anyway. That cave would be the place where the whole Chaos series originated. It makes sense."

"So all we have to do is find this cave that may or may not exist," Joe said. "I wonder if this'd be any easier if I'd played the third game."

After breakfast Joe, Frank, and Chelsea showered in shifts, dressed, and headed for Viking Software.

When they got there, Chelsea introduced Phil to Dave Henderson, her boss. Dave seemed upset about the whole situation.

"It's like some nightmare I can't wake up from," he said. "Like being trapped in one of Royal's games."

"That's the way I felt last night when that driverless car tried to run Frank and Joe down," Chelsea said.

"Chelsea," Joe said, "you mentioned something about A Town Called Chaos when Royal's sedan tried to hit us last night. Is there a driverless car in the new game?"

"Yes. Along with a giant ape, exploding bats, a

booby-trapped mansion, the ghost of Katherine Chaos's evil sister, and a lot of other cool things. Seeing something like that real car doesn't seem so cool, though," Chelsea said.

"And the giant spider was in the second game," Joe said. "What kind of things from the third game might we find in this forest?"

"You're going to Kendall Forest?" Chelsea and Phil asked simultaneously.

"Right after we get Phil set up here. It seems the only logical thing to do," Frank said.

"Well . . ." Chelsea said, thinking, "there were a lot of things from the first two games: more spiders, more snakes, and, of course, the Terrible Bear—the one Tochi thinks is a parody of Bombo."

"I don't know about this," Dave said. "I'm pretty nervous about you guys poking around in the woods. Shouldn't we leave this to the police?"

"The police think your company is behind this whole thing," Joe said. "They're still concentrating on the publicity stunt theory."

"Well, if I can track down where those first e-mails actually came from, maybe we can stop that," Phil said.

"I'll take you to a workstation," Dave said. He led the Hardys and Phil to an empty cubicle. Chelsea went back to her office. Even on a Saturday morning, Viking Software bustled with energy. Several projects were so close to their deadlines that nearly everyone on staff was working overtime.

Frank and Joe helped Phil get set up, then they headed out to the van to begin their trip north to Kendall State Park. But when they got into the Viking Software parking lot, the door of a red Volkswagen Beetle opened up next to them and out climbed Samantha Rockford. Apparently, she'd been waiting for them.

"So," Sam said, strolling up to the brothers and falling into step beside them, "what's our next move?"

"What do you mean 'our'? " Frank asked.

"And where did you hurry off to last night?" Joe said. "I think the police might want to talk to you."

"I try never to become involved with police," Sam said. "Look," she continued. "I figure you and I should team up. You guys got to this case ahead of me, but I probably know a lot more about Royal than you do. I've studied him. I know all his friends and acquaintances, all his usual haunts."

"Then," Frank said, trying to walk away from her, "you should have no trouble finding him on your own."

"Hey," she said, tagging along, "we're all on the same side here."

"If we're all on the same side," Joe said, "let's see your PI's license."

Sam's eyes narrowed. "Let's see yours."

Frank stopped walking and looked Sam straight in the eyes. She was wearing the same cheap thirties detective outfit she'd worn the night before, he noticed. "Personally," he said, "I'd settle for seeing just your ID."

"I left it at home," Sam said. "I never carry ID when I work. It might compromise my employers."

"A likely story," Joe said.

Just then Chelsea Sirkin came out of the front door of the building. "Frank, Joe, you'll never guess what I found," she said. Then, noticing the woman in the trench coat and fedora, she added, "Oh. I'm sorry. Who's your friend?"

Joe stepped aside so Chelsea could get a better look at Sam. "Chelsea Sirkin, I'd like you to meet the ubiquitous Samantha Rockford."

Chelsea's jaw dropped open. Looking straight at Sam, she gasped, "What are *you* doing here?"

# 9 Samantha's Secret

"She's trying to tag along with us," Joe said. "But I don't think we're buying."

"B-but her name's not Rockford, and she's not a PI!" Chelsea stammered. "Her real name is Teri McLean, and she's a fan who's been stalking Royal for years."

McLean turned to run, but Joe grabbed her by the wrist and held tight. "Oh, no," he said. "You're not going to pull that disappearing act again."

"You've got nothing on me," McLean said. "Let me go or I'll scream for the cops."

"She's wrong about that," Chelsea said. "We've got enough for the cops to hold her. Royal took out a restraining order against Teri that prevents her from being this close to him, his house, or his place of work. She's in violation of that order right now."

"Guess you aren't as innocent as you pretend," Joe said.

Teri didn't reply, only tried to slide out of Joe's grip. Joe had to use some of his wrestling skills to keep hold of her, but he didn't let her get away. After a while, she gave up and stopped struggling.

Chelsea was angry now. "You bet she isn't innocent. She used to follow Anne Sakai around, too. Royal says that this woman is the reason Sakai left the country before she died."

"So, you're saying that if it wasn't for Ms. Sweetness-and-Light here, Sakai might not have died in that plane crash?" Frank asked.

"That's a lie!" Teri McLean screamed. "Anne and I were good friends. She invited me down to that island!"

"You were on St. Cecile before Anne Sakai died?" Chelsea asked, wide-eyed.

A cold calm passed over McLean, and her whole attitude changed. "I'm not saying anything more," she said.

"I wouldn't clam up now if I were you," Frank said. "You're in enough trouble as it is. You'd better come clean if you hope to get out of this."

McLean didn't say anything, and Joe, who still had her by the wrist, began to pull her back toward the Viking Software building. As they neared the door, McLean suddenly yanked free and dashed to the red VW. She started to tug the door open, but Frank stopped her. "Going somewhere?" he asked.

"You can't stop me," she said. As she pulled on the door, something fell out of the pocket of her trench coat. She scooped up the item but not before Frank and Joe saw what it was: a fairly new set of lock picks. McLean glared angrily at the brothers. "This is illegal detainment," she said.

"On the contrary," Joe said, stepping in behind her. "We're just holding you for the police." McLean was now trapped between her VW and the car next to it, with the Hardys cutting off her only avenues of escape.

She tried to yank open the door again, but Frank stopped her. "Let me go, you two!" she cried. "Steven's life is in danger! I'm the only one who can save him!"

"I doubt that," Joe said. Then something in the Beetle caught his eye. "Hey, Frank. Take a look inside the car."

Frank looked in, being careful not to let McLean slip away. The floor of the vehicle was strewn with papers; some of them had Steven Royal's letterhead on them, others bore the seal of NCU. "I think," he said, "we may have found out who ransacked Royal's condo and Tochi's house—it looks like she took a few souvenirs."

"I didn't ransack anything," McLean complained. "Those aren't souvenirs, they're clues. You'd have done the same thing."

"No, we wouldn't," Joe said. "And we'll let the police decide if those papers are evidence in this case, or evidence that you're a thief."

Frank smiled grimly at McLean. "I think you may have some trouble explaining the lock picks. If you were better at using them, you'd have left fewer clues."

"I'll get security," Chelsea said, heading for the building.

"You've got to listen to me," McLean said. "I didn't do anything wrong. I'm only trying to help Steven Royal. He's in big trouble, I just know it. He'd never disappear like this before the release of a big game. He needs that game."

"Needs it how?" Joe asked.

McLean looked around furtively, then said, "He's almost broke. He made some bad investments."

"And I suppose you learned that from some of those papers in your car," Frank said.

"It doesn't matter how I know," McLean said. "I was just trying to protect him, but it didn't work. Something terrible has happened to him, I just know it. I'm looking out for him. . . ."

"Following him, you mean," Joe interjected.

"He slipped away from me last Monday," McLean continued, "and he never came back. Didn't he know I was just trying to protect him?"

"Was he driving his car when he got away?" asked Frank.

"Yes," McLean said. "He was heading north, but he lost me on an interchange. I think he did it deliberately. I didn't know anything was wrong until he didn't come back for a few days. That was when I decided to take things into my own hands."

"So, you used those lock picks and looked around in his place, and Tochi's, just trying to protect Royal," Joe said.

"Yes. I know he's in trouble. He's been nervous lately, but I don't know why. I just want to help."

"I'm sure you do," Frank said. McLean had become calmer, and he hoped to get more information out of her before the police arrived. "So, what do you think happened to him?"

"Anne Sakai's ghost got him," McLean said matter-of-factly.

Both Hardys tried not to look shocked. "Sakai's ghost?" Joe asked skeptically.

McLean crossed her arms over her chest. "She's out to get him for driving her out of the country. She decided she couldn't compete with him, so she ran away. Then she got killed. So her ghost blames him for it. Now she's done something terrible to him."

"And you've actually . . . *seen* this ghost?" Frank asked.

"Only once," McLean said quietly. "After she died on St. Cecile."

Just then Chelsea returned with the building security guard. He took custody of McLean and escorted her into the building to wait for the police.

"So," Joe said watching her go, "do you think she did something to Royal?"

Frank shook his head. "I doubt it—though I couldn't rule it out. I think it's more likely that she had something to do with Sakai's death. She confessed to being on the island around the time of Sakai's plane crash."

"Do you think Sakai took that fatal plane trip to get away from her?" Joe asked.

"Could be," Frank said. "We know McLean followed Sakai all the way to the Caribbean. What we don't know is, why? Is she just a crazy fan, or was she trying to get in good with Royal? Maybe she sabotaged the plane somehow. With Sakai out of the picture, the Chaos series is all Royal's."

"Oh!" Chelsea said. "That's one of the things I came out to tell you. This business with McLean had me so rattled, I almost forgot.

"You asked about Sakai's heirs the other day,"

she continued. "I checked and she did have one heir, Regina Cross. Sakai's proceeds from the Chaos games go to Cross Enterprises in Switzerland. She has a piece of all three games, but I'm not sure about the new game.

"That's the other thing I needed to tell you. Dave turned up something funny in Royal's contract. Just a few weeks ago Royal had a minor change made."

"What change?" Frank asked.

"Well, on the last contract anyone who helped Royal with the programming for the game was paid directly by Viking Software. Now, though, Royal is the only one we pay, and then he pays anyone who works under him. Since he didn't have any collaborators, our lawyers didn't think it was a big deal to change it."

"No collaborators that you *know* of," Joe said, frowning.

"Can you find out if Sakai's heir, Cross, has a stake in the new game?" asked Frank.

"Sure," Chelsea said.

"We'd better get going," Joe said. "It'll be dark by the time we get back."

Frank nodded and both of them headed toward the van. "We'll keep in touch," he called back. Chelsea waved as she walked back into the building.

❖　❖　❖

84

Three hours later the Hardys pulled off the main road and onto one of the trails crisscrossing Kendall State Park. The man at the gatehouse couldn't tell them where to find the cave. He said that many people had searched for it before, but never found it. Personally, he thought it was just a myth. He wished the brothers well and gave them a map of the park.

Getting some help from Chelsea on their car phone, the Hardys picked a parking spot in a location that seemed to match the geography of the Chaos games.

"You know," Joe said as he got out of the van and hefted his backpack, "I wish I'd played Forest of Chaos. It might have helped now that we're in the same woods."

The two of them consulted their map and picked a trail that would take them by the Kendall River. "There was a river in the game," Joe said. "It flowed through the cave. It's not much of a lead, but it may be our best shot."

"Any monsters in the river?" Frank asked.

"Yeah. Some kind of cave octopus thing."

"Well," Frank said, adjusting his backpack, "let's hope we don't run into it."

"You know, if we can find an eagle head–shaped rock we should be able to find the cave—" He stopped abruptly to glance back toward the parking lot.

"What is it?" asked Frank.

"I thought I saw another car," Joe said. "It's gone now."

"Probably just sightseers," Frank said. "This place is beautiful."

"Well, it won't be as beautiful when it gets dark in a couple of hours," Joe said. The two of them walked in silence for a while after that, Joe keeping his eyes peeled for any landmark clues from the games.

Suddenly Frank stopped.

"What is it?" Joe asked.

"Shh! Listen."

Joe listened and heard a faint rustling in the woods behind them. He and Frank turned and looked.

About thirty yards away, through the under-brush, they could just make out the form of a huge gray wolf.

"He's stalking us!" whispered Frank.

# 10 The Cave of Chaos

"I've got my pocketknife," Joe said softly. "And a hand ax in my backpack."

"Not enough," Frank replied. "Maybe we could take him, but we'd get badly mauled in the process."

"No way we can make it back to the van," Joe said. "Look at the way he moves through the woods."

"He's lived here all his life, probably," Frank said. "Though I don't remember gray wolves being in this part of Massachusetts."

"Well, one's here now," Joe said. "At least he's not closing in."

"Not yet, anyway. If we can't go back, we should press to look for shelter. Come on, Joe. We'll just keep a careful eye on him."

"I'll keep *two* careful eyes on him," Joe said.

The Hardys ventured deeper into the woods. Occasionally, they would spot the wolf trailing them, or ranging off to one side. All at once, though, the creature was in front of them, barring their path.

He stood on the path about a hundred yards away from the brothers, growling menacingly.

"Looks like this is the end of the road," Frank said. "Unless you want to tackle Tall, Dark, and Furry."

"At least he's not a bear," Joe replied. "Chelsea said there were bears in Forest of Chaos."

"Well, I don't want to fight either a wolf or a bear if we can help it—unless, of course, it was Bombo Bear," Frank said. "I've got a feeling Bombo would be a pushover."

Despite the tense situation, the quip brought a smile to Joe's lips. As Frank watched the wolf, Joe checked their map. "If we leave the trail here," Joe said, "I think we can still get to the river."

"I guess that's our best bet," said Frank. "Assuming Mr. Fuzzy agrees."

Joe nodded and the two left the path and stepped into the woods. Joe fished out his compass. "You know, I'd love to have one of those Global Positioning Systems right about now," he said.

"I'd settle for a phone," Frank said.

The wolf didn't move any closer, but the brothers could still see him through the woods, ranging off to their left. Kendall State Park was quiet for the summer, Frank thought. The only noise was the sound of their footsteps, the soft padding of the wolf, and the whistle of an occasional bird.

As the sun started to dip low in the sky, the Hardys continued to play cat and mouse with the wolf. The wolf didn't get any closer to them, nor did he veer away. He seemed to be watching and waiting.

"You know," Joe said after a while, "that doesn't look like any wolf I've ever seen before."

"Yeah," Frank agreed. "I was thinking the same thing. His face isn't shaped quite right. Maybe he's a wolf-dog hybrid. Sometimes people keep hybrids as pets."

"And sometimes they get loose," added Joe. "That'd explain what a wolf is doing in this part of the country. Guess that's why they have leash laws."

Frank cocked his head. "Joe, do you hear that?"

Joe did the same. "Those birds singing?" he asked.

"Not that," Frank said.

Joe listened again, harder this time. "Running water. The river. Sounds pretty close. I didn't notice it before."

"Let's go," Frank said.

The wolf-dog didn't prevent them from reaching the water. Kendall River was about twenty feet wide and ran swiftly, babbling over numerous rocks and small boulders.

"Good whitewater, if it's deep enough," Joe said.

"Mm," Frank said. With his eyes, he was tracing a line of boulders that crossed the river. "Hey, Joe," he said, pointing. "What's that look like to you?"

Joe looked where Frank indicated. In the woods nearby a large configuration of jumbled rocks cropped up out of the ground. From where the Hardys stood, the rock formation looked like the profile of a huge bird.

"Wow," Joe said. "I'd say that must be Eagle Rock. According to the information Chelsea gave me, the eagle's head is supposed to point toward the Cave of Chaos."

Frank squinted and peered into the woods. "I think I do see a large rocky mound that way," he said. "Let's try it. Keep an eye on that wolf, though."

The Hardys cautiously made their way through the woods to the rock mound. It jutted out of the landscape like the back of a whale. Several smaller boulders lay beside its base, but to one side of the mound the brothers could see an opening just big enough for a person to squeeze through.

"That's it!" Joe said. "We've found it!"

Frank glanced back the way they had come. He didn't see anything, and when he listened, all he heard was the faint singing of birds. "I think our wolfish friend has given up on us," he said.

"You know," Joe said. "We ought to thank that wolf. If we hadn't left the path, I doubt we'd have ever spotted Eagle Rock."

Frank and Joe squeezed inside the opening. Just beyond the entrance, the cave opened up into a small "room," with one narrow passageway leading back deeper into the rock.

"Did you notice those boulders near the entrance?" Frank asked.

"Yeah," Joe replied. "Looked like they'd been moved recently: the ground around them was disturbed and the moss was growing on the wrong side of them. What I wonder is, who moved them and why?"

"Maybe to open up the entrance to the cave. Those boulders could have prevented anyone from discovering it," Frank said.

"I suppose one guy could have moved them with a decent lever," Joe said.

"Royal, you mean," Frank said. "The question now is, is there anything in here, or is he just leading us on a wild-goose chase?"

"Only one way to find out," said Joe. He pulled his flashlight from his backpack and switched it on. Then he and Frank ventured into the passageway beyond the room.

"Looks like a glacial cave," Joe said, running his hand over one rough wall. "Formed by the movements of rocks during the last ice age."

"Yeah," Frank said. "Nothing like Carlsbad, or the Cave of the Mounds. No stalactites or stalagmites. Pretty big for a glacial system, though."

"Not too big, I hope," Joe said. "I'd still like to get out of here before dark. Hey, Frank, I've been thinking."

"Yeah?"

"About something Chelsea said earlier. Didn't she mention the ghost of Katherine Chaos's sister being in the new game?"

"I think so," Frank said. His eyes lit up. "Are you thinking that maybe McLean isn't so crazy after all?"

Joe nodded. "We know that she couldn't have seen a ghost, but maybe she did see someone who *looked* like Sakai."

"A relative, you mean," Frank said. "I wonder if Regina Cross is related to Sakai. Usually people's heirs are their relatives."

Suddenly Joe stopped walking. "Of course, it may not matter."

"What do you mean?" Frank asked, shifting his gaze from his brother to where Joe's light was shining into another "room" ahead of them. His eyes followed the flashlight beam to a gold disk resting atop a small pillar of rocks. "The prototype disk!" they said, and rushed into the chamber. With their flashlights, they could even pick out words printed on the disk in plain block lettering: "A Town Called Chaos: Master."

Just then a loud hissing caught the Hardys' attention. Not more than two yards away, a large yellowish snake sat coiled and poised to strike.

"Cobra!" Joe whispered.

"In this cold, damp climate?" Frank said. "I don't think so. Stay here." He took a few steps back down the tunnel and picked up a large rock with both hands.

"What are you going to do if you're wrong," Joe asked, glancing nervously from Frank to the snake and then back again.

"Run," Frank said. "And try to figure out a better plan. Do something to distract it, will you?"

Joe tossed his flashlight near the snake. As the reptile turned toward it, Frank heaved his rock at the cobra. The snake reacted, but not in time; Frank's rock hit it with a loud crunch.

Frank and Joe stepped carefully forward, making sure no more snakes were around. Joe leaned down to retrieve his flashlight and examine the carcass. He picked up the snake's tail; a few bits of metal and small gears fell out of it. "Mechanical," he said. "Just like the spider."

"I thought so," Frank said. "I would have been surprised if there wasn't one last trap before the treasure."

"So, let's get the disk and vamoose," Joe said. He sauntered forward and plucked the golden computer CD from its resting place. He turned back toward Frank and smiled, holding the disk up.

As he did, the chamber began to shake. Dust fell from the ceiling and a low rumbling sound filled the space.

"Look out, Frank!" Joe cried.

Frank turned in time to see a huge boulder separate from the other rocks above the entranceway to the chamber. The boulder fell straight toward him.

# 11 Treasure and Treachery

Frank dove toward Joe, and the boulder missed him by inches. It did, however, seal off the entrance to the chamber. Frank and Joe put their shoulders to the rock, but it was too heavy to move.

"A pretty shoddy way to treat your publisher's agents," Frank noted.

"There must have been some kind of trigger system connected to the disk," Joe said. "I should have looked."

"No sense worrying about it now," Frank said. "I thought we'd seen the last of Royal's tricks as well."

"Well, this one seems pretty final to me," Joe said. "I don't see any way out of this cave."

Frank looked around. Joe was right. The chamber they were in appeared to be a dead end. "I can't believe that Royal would lead us all the way here just to trap us," Frank said. "What would be the point?"

"Maybe he thought he'd be trapping someone else," said Joe.

"Could be. But with all the careful planning that's gone into this scheme, why leave to chance who gets trapped? If it was someone who worked with him, or one of his old 'friends,' I'd understand. But I can't believe we could get this far without his knowing it was us—or at least, that we weren't who he expected."

"Yeah. Seems crazy to set up a complicated game like this and not know who's playing against you." Joe stooped to examine the pillar that had held the CD. He uncovered a transmitter unit. "Here's what set off the trap. More technology. If Tochi was right about Royal's skills, someone else *must* have helped him set all this up."

"Maybe Tochi himself, you think?" Frank asked. "He seems most likely. Could be he and Royal have made up and are working on some kind of video game together—despite what Tochi said."

"Or maybe," Joe said as he continued to check the pillar, "whoever did this doesn't want us to be trapped here forever . . . Frank, there's a wire attached to this pillar and it runs down into the rock."

"How could that be unless . . ."

Joe smiled. "The rock isn't really rock at all." He gently wobbled the rock pillar back and forth.

"Careful, Joe," Frank said.

"I will be," Joe replied. "Though I don't see how things could get much worse." A few more wobbles and the pillar broke off in Joe's hands. "Plaster," he said. "Painted to look like the surrounding rock."

"The wire continues out the bottom. Part of the floor must be plaster, too," Frank said.

Joe nodded and took his hand ax out of his backpack. Frank did the same. Together they methodically chipped the painted plaster away from the floor until they found the wire, which led into the wall.

"Do you think the wall could be fake, too?" Joe asked.

"Only one way to find out."

The brothers attacked the wall with their axes. Sure enough, part of it was plaster as well. Soon they'd chipped a hole big enough for both of them to get out. They went through the hole, following the exposed wire into a larger tunnel beyond the fake wall. The wire led to a large battery hidden in a small niche on the other side of the wall.

"You know," Joe said as they stood up in the passage beyond the wall, "if I'd been thinking, I would have remembered that there are a lot of fake walls in the Chaos games. That battery must have powered the trap."

Frank nodded. "It was still a pretty dangerous stunt. That rock might have crushed us." He checked the compass from his backpack. "This passage seems to head back the way we came," he said. "Let's hope it leads out."

Joe nodded and the two set off down the tunnel. Soon, they emerged into the cool night air near Eagle Rock. "I hope that wolf-dog isn't still around," Joe said.

"I'd be surprised if he is," Frank said. "I have a feeling his job is done."

"You think he was part of Royal's plan?" Joe asked.

"Think about it. He chased us all the way to the cave and then took off. Plus, now that I'm thinking about it, those bird songs I heard earlier were awfully strange."

"You're right," Joe said. "I was too concerned about the wolf to notice at the time, but they could have been command whistles—like people use when they train dogs."

"So we were being led by the nose during this whole game," Frank said, kicking a rock in frustration. "Come on, let's get back to the van. At least the game is over."

"And we won," Joe added.

An hour later the Hardys reached the parking area where they'd left their van. They opened the back door and flopped inside, exhausted. It was night by then, and starlit darkness shrouded the New England woods.

After resting for a few minutes, they climbed into their seats and headed south toward Jewel Ridge. Joe called Viking Software while Frank drove. When Phil answered the phone, Joe put it on the speaker.

"Hey, great to hear from you guys," he said. "How'd it go?"

"Well, it looked pretty hairy for a while," Joe said, "but everything turned out fine in the end. We've got the master disk."

"That's great," Phil said. "I dug up something on those computer messages, too."

"It can wait," Frank said. "Now that we've got the disk, it doesn't much matter where Royal is. I'm sure he'll turn up now that his little game is over."

"And when he does show," Joe added, "I hope the cops give it to him. And if they don't, I will.

99

His stunts could have gotten someone hurt—or worse."

"Yell at him all you want, as long as it doesn't mess up the release of the game," Phil said. "Look, we'll see you when you get here."

"Right," Joe said, and hung up the phone. They stopped on the way back for burgers and gas but otherwise drove straight through. Still, it was close to one A.M. when they finally arrived at the offices of Viking Software.

Dave, Chelsea, and Phil were a small welcoming committee and gave the Hardys an ovation as the brothers dragged themselves in. "Thank you. Thank you so much," Dave said, beaming.

Phil clapped each of his friends on the shoulder, and Chelsea gave each a big hug and a kiss on the cheek. "How can we ever reward you?" she asked.

"A hot bath, a good meal, and a good night's sleep," Joe replied. He handed the master disk to her.

"Come on," Phil said, waving to the cubicle where he'd been working. "I've got everything set up to check out the disk."

Dave looked worried. "You don't think it might be the wrong disk, do you? After all this?"

"We won't know until we try it," Frank said. Like Joe, he was exhausted.

Phil sat down at the workstation, and Chelsea

handed him the disk. They popped it into the DVD/CD drive, and the computer hummed to life.

A moment later the game filled the screen with dazzling graphics. Bats swooped and screeched over a deserted town, and somewhere in the distance a church bell tolled thirteen. Then suddenly a building exploded and the title of the game appeared on the screen: A Town Called Chaos.

"Yes!" Dave said, jumping up and giving Chelsea a high-five.

Soon, the Katherine Chaos character appeared on screen. First, there was a brief but visually stunning recap of the first three games, then an explanation of the goal of the game: to lift the curse of Chaos from Katherine's hometown.

Then the intro ended, and the game demo began.

"These graphics are amazing!" Joe said. "Light-years beyond the first two games."

"I've never seen these sequences before," Dave said, hardly daring to take his eyes from the screen.

"I have," Chelsea said, smiling from ear to ear. "The last time I saw Royal. These are the missing sequences. Frank and Joe, you did it! Viking Software is saved!"

"Let's see how it plays," Phil said. He hit the control key to stop the demo and start the game.

Suddenly the screen went blank. The computer's drives whirred madly, and then the screen filled with a rapidly changing series of ones and zeros.

Both Chelsea and Phil went pale. "Computer virus!" they gasped.

# 12 The Past Is the Future

"Do something!" Dave said, practically screaming.

"I'm trying, I'm trying," said Phil, frantically pounding the keyboard.

"Phil!" Chelsea said, tension making her voice shrill.

A few seconds later Phil stopped typing. "It's okay," he said. "Everything's okay. I stopped it before it could do any damage to the Viking systems."

Joe clapped him on the back. "Good work, Phil."

Phil leaned back in his chair. "Actually, I was half expecting something like this. With all the games Royal's put you guys through, I thought he might have a trick or two left. So I put up a fire wall between this computer and the rest of the system. Good thing, too. This virus is one of the nastiest I've ever seen. That Royal must be one amazing programmer."

"Actually," Frank said, "I think this little stunt proves that Royal isn't behind our present troubles."

"He's not?" Dave and Chelsea asked simultaneously.

"Think about it," Joe said. "What would Royal have to gain from wrecking your system? It won't get him out of his contract with you, will it?"

"It might if it put us out of business," Dave said. "But I think we'd have a pretty good case against him if that happened now."

"So do I," Frank said. "And I don't think Royal's dumb enough to think otherwise. No, from all the evidence we have now, and from what's happened here tonight, I think it's pretty clear that we've been barking up the wrong tree. Steven Royal isn't running this game, and he hasn't been from the beginning."

"So, who is?" Chelsea asked.

"We can't be sure, yet," Joe said. "Obviously it's someone out to ruin Royal's work and reputation. Rosenberg, Tochi, and Winters are still the obvious suspects. All could benefit from the failure of the new Chaos game and, incidentally, Viking Software."

"There may be another suspect, too," Phil said. "Remember last night I said I'd turned up something new? Well, I traced both those computer messages you found to a computer in Switzerland, just over the Italian border."

"Near Italy?" Joe asked. "That could mean that Tochi's involved. His family comes from there."

"There's more," Phil said. "The computer I traced the messages to is owned by Cross Enterprises."

"Sakai's heir?" asked Dave.

"Looks like," Frank said. "Now things are starting to fall into place. Remember when McLean told us she'd seen Sakai's ghost? Well, suppose it wasn't a ghost, but a look-alike relative, Regina Cross. Could be that relative blames Royal for Sakai's death. Trashing Royal's rep might be the best way to get back at him."

"But Sakai's heirs would still get money from any game in the Chaos series," Phil said. "Smearing Royal would be like throwing money out the window."

Dave cut in. "Not on the game we're putting out now. I checked on that. So far as I know, the Crosses don't get any cut at all," he said. "Royal is the only person we're obligated to pay under our contract, and then Royal pays anyone who works with him."

"That's what the recent contract change did,"

Frank said. "And I'm betting that that's what set this all off. Royal disappeared last Monday, shortly after he made that change to the contract."

"Whoever he was working with kidnapped him," Joe said.

"But that still doesn't tell us where he is, or who's behind this," Chelsea said. "You really think he's been kidnapped?"

"It seems pretty likely now," Joe said. "Though I'm not sure the police would think so."

"At least they're looking for him, because of that remote-controlled car bit," said Frank. "Say, did anyone follow up on that?"

"Chelsea and I poked around in the police files," Phil said. "Their preliminary report says that the control unit was made up of common electronic components, processors from toys, and parts of an old amusement park ride—chain-belts, gears, things like that."

"An amusement park ride?" said Joe. "Hmm. This puzzle has too many pieces."

"But I'm betting," Frank said, "that with a little bit of work, we can put them all together. We're all going to be up late tonight, but I think we're finally on the right track. Here's what I want everyone to do . . ."

Frank divided the group up and gave each person a specific task. They each used a computer to search. They took catnaps when they couldn't keep their eyes open, but they didn't nap long before going back to work. By morning they had a good deal to go on—though no one had gotten enough sleep.

Dave called the tired-looking group together in a conference room early Sunday morning. "Okay," he said. "What did everyone find out?"

"Looks like Winters is in the clear," Joe said. "After he sped away from our little tussle the other night, he got caught for speeding in the next county. He must have had a lot of outstanding tickets because they're still holding him at the county jail. He couldn't have been messing with us since then."

Joe continued. "McLean is under psychiatric observation. I think they're looking at giving her a one-way ticket. What about Tochi?"

"His record looks clean," Frank said, "though McLean's breaking into his place did make the police blotter. Otherwise, he's got an outstanding record."

"He still seems like one of the best candidates," Joe said. "He'd have the expertise to make those mechanical animals. Bombo was a pretty impressive toy, at least mechanically. I wonder why he sicced that wolf-dog on us in the woods, though? If he's our culprit it seems to me that he'd have wanted to use a bear."

"Maybe all the bears were booked up," Phil said.

"Wolf-dog?" Chelsea said. "I remember reading something about that when I was researching Royal's past. Anne Sakai had a dog that was part wolf. I wonder what became of it after she died."

"I think I know," Dave said. "I checked into the public records of Sakai's will. It seems she didn't have a very large estate when she died. She had gotten into some tax trouble. The IRS got what they could, but they think that she probably had some untraceable Swiss bank accounts."

"Cross Enterprises is in Switzerland," Joe said.

Dave nodded. "Yes."

"How long before she died did Sakai write the will?" Frank asked.

"Funny thing, she only wrote it about a week before she died. She filed it and had it notarized on the island. And, in her will, Sakai left her dog, Scavenger, to Regina Cross—who the will says *is* her cousin. But as near as I can figure out, the dog never left the U.S. There was some kind of trouble about taking a half-wolf to Europe. So the dog stayed in this country, in a kennel—until someone picked him up, about two months after Sakai's death. I tracked down the kennel records over the Net."

"Do you think you could see if that dog has been kenneled recently?" Frank asked.

"I'll get right on it," Dave said, and left the room.

"You know, if we get good enough at this, we might be able to crack all our cases from the comfort of our computer room back home," Joe said.

"This case isn't cracked yet," Frank said. "And besides, where's the fun in that?"

"You know," Phil said, "I've got a funny idea. Sometimes skills run in families—for example, Chelsea and I are both good with computers."

"I see where you're going, and I've been thinking the same thing," Frank said. "Sakai was good with computers and all kinds of machines. Maybe that knack runs in her family."

"Which would make Regina Cross—Sakai's cousin—the perfect person to pull off a scheme like this," Joe said. "Which also fits in with McLean's 'ghost' theory."

"That's not all," Chelsea said. "I cross-referenced the names of all the people with that name in the United States. One of them lives in Sullivan's Point, up in New Hampshire. And, according to the research I did, Sullivan's Point is where Anne Sakai grew up."

"Here's the kicker," Phil said. "Among the papers in McLean's car that the police confiscated was one that indicated that Royal hired Cross Enterprises to work on parts of A Town Called Chaos."

"Which means Royal had complete control over how Cross Enterprises was paid, according to his recent contract change," said Frank. "So he could change their deal at any time. Suppose he decided to pay her less than they had agreed. He could do that legally now."

"I'd say that jumps Regina Cross to the head of our suspects list," Joe said. "Maybe she and Royal had a disagreement over money. Or maybe she's been carrying a grudge about what happened to her cousin. Or maybe she just doesn't like him—a lot of people apparently don't."

Just then Dave came back into the room. "Guys, I've found it," he said. "A dog by that name and matching the description has been kenneled in Benson, New Hampshire, off and on for the last few years and as recently as a month ago."

"I bet if we check a map," Joe said, "that Benson will turn out to be close to Sullivan's Point."

"We can check the map in the car," Frank said. "Let's go."

"Can we stop for a shower at Chelsea's place first?" Joe asked. "If I'm going to face down danger, I'd rather not be Mr. Grunge."

An hour later, washed and fed, Frank and Joe Hardy rolled out of Jewel Ridge on their way to Sullivan's Point, New Hampshire. Locating the town didn't turn out to be as easy as they had expected; it wasn't on the map in their car, but Phil turned it up on an older map he found on the Internet.

"Strange the town isn't on our map," Joe said.

"Almost par for the course on this case," Frank noted. "We're looking for a 'ghost' in a town that doesn't exist."

The two had left Chelsea, Phil, and Dave to hold the fort at Viking Software. They were also going to explain the Hardys' theory of the case to the local police. Frank figured the explanations would take someone, probably Dave, most of the day, and even then he didn't expect the police to believe their theory.

Sullivan's Point was located in the mountainous northwest corner of New Hampshire. Driving there took the Hardys most of the day. As they drove they kept in touch with Phil and Chelsea via their car phone. Late in the afternoon, Phil had some news for them.

"I found out why Sullivan's Point isn't on any map," he said. "It's a ghost town. The economy of the place collapsed fifteen years ago, and everybody moved away."

"There's at least one person still living there," Joe said. "Two, I hope."

"I hope so, too," Chelsea added, chiming in over the speakerphone. "We still need that game, or Viking is sunk. But I hope Royal's okay, too.

He's not as bad as people have been painting him."

"One more thing," Phil said. "In the last two years, a corporation has bought up all the available land in the town. Care to guess which corporation?"

"On a wild hunch, I'd have to say Cross Enterprises," Frank said.

"Bingo," Phil agreed. "Guys, be careful."

"We will be," Frank assured him.

As they neared the outskirts of Benson, Frank and Joe stopped for gas and to confirm their directions to Sullivan's Point.

"Good thing you stopped by," said the grizzled gas station attendant. "There's a bridge on this road that washed out last winter. You'll have to take the mountain road into town. Don't know why you'd want to go, though. Nobody there but ghosts and crazy people."

"We're looking for someone," said Joe. "Maybe you've seen her. Her name's Regina Cross."

"Oh yeah," the old man said, "I know her—athletic blond, good looking, always wears sunglasses. Didn't mean what I said about her being crazy. She's just a bit . . . eccentric. She brings her SUV into town every month or so to pick up gas and supplies. Haven't seen her for a while, though."

The man scratched his head, "Funny thing," he said. "You're the second people asking after Regina and Sullivan's Point in the last couple weeks."

"Who else was asking?" Joe asked.

"Didn't catch his name," the man said. "Drove a big blue car. He was in an awful hurry, pretty rude, too. Seemed to think he owned the world."

Frank and Joe looked at each other. "Royal," they said simultaneously.

The Hardys piled back into the van and followed the directions the old man had given them. A few miles out of town they passed an abandoned amusement park: "Lincoln Park—Home of the Terrifying Giganto." The head was broken off the Giganto sign, so the Hardys couldn't tell what kind of a hairy monster Giganto had been. The skeleton of a roller coaster decorated the far skyline.

"Nice place for picking up spare parts," Frank noted.

"You mean like the ones the police found in the wreck of Royal's car," Joe said. "I bet if we checked, we'd find out Cross Enterprises owns what's left of that park."

Soon after that, the land around them rose and the brothers found themselves driving through thickly wooded hills. The condition of the road deteriorated quickly, until the "highway" was little more than a dirt road.

"Guess ghosts don't pay enough taxes to get good roadwork done," Joe said.

In a short time they topped a hill and gazed down into Sullivan's Point. Anne Sakai's hometown was a spooky place, full of rapidly decaying century-old buildings. The sun was sinking behind the hills as the Hardys drove into town, and late-afternoon shadows crept through the town's deserted streets.

Joe turned from the abandoned church nearby to gaze at a dilapidated mansion on the far side of town. "Nice place for a horror movie," he said.

"There's a light in that mansion," Frank said. "Top window. Do you see it?"

Joe nodded. "There's always a light on over at the Frankenstein place. Think she knows we're coming?"

"She might," Frank said. "We'll have to watch ourselves."

As he said it, the sky above them suddenly grew dark. Hordes of huge black bats began streaming out of the bell tower of the old church. The creatures wheeled and gyrated in the sky, gathering like a huge swarm of hornets.

A few bats broke off from the group and hurled themselves at the Hardys' van. Frank cut the wheel just in time to avoid having a bat splatter on the windshield.

But instead of splattering, the bat exploded in a ball of orange-yellow fire as it hit the ground.

At the sound of the explosion, the rest of the bats turned toward the Hardys' van and dove straight toward it.

# 13 A Town Called Chaos

"Exploding bats!" Joe cried.

"I see them, I see them," Frank said as he twisted the steering wheel to avoid the first wave of the attacking creatures.

The bats whirled around the van, chittering and screeching. Most of them flitted away at the last moment, but a few came straight in, like kamikaze bombers.

Frank tried to avoid the squadron, but the rough condition of the road made it difficult. When he cut the wheel one way, the ruts in the road would take his tires in another direction. Several of the exploding bats hit the sides of the van, but they did no significant damage.

Frank cut the wheel and a bat caught the edge

of the windshield, skitted down the side window, and exploded. The blast cracked one of the van's rear windows.

"Yow! That was too close," said Joe.

"How about coming up with a plan while I drive," Frank said, tense concentration filling his voice. Joe could see beads of sweat running down his brother's forehead. Frank's face was set in a grim, determined-looking mask.

"Do we still have that fishing net?" Joe asked.

"Maybe under the backseat," Frank said. "Be careful."

Joe unbuckled himself and moved toward the back of the van. It was like trying to walk on a ship during a storm, and Joe had to clutch the backs of the seats to keep his balance.

Suddenly a huge explosion made the van lurch wildly.

"Hang on!" Frank shouted. "I think they got the tires!"

Joe grabbed the nearest seat belt, wrapped it around his wrist, and hung on for dear life.

Frank fought for control of the van, but something more than the tires had gone. The bats continued to scream around the van, obscuring his vision. Occasionally, one exploded in a puff of flame and black smoke.

Suddenly a huge oak tree loomed out of the cloud of bats. Frank turned left with all his might.

The van skidded, and hit the tree with its side. Every loose object in the van flew into the air at the impact. The van swerved the other way, almost tipping over. Finally it lurched into a ditch and came to a stop.

Frank shook his head to clear it. "Joe! Are you all right?"

"I've been better." Joe's voice came from under a seat that had shaken loose in the crash.

Another explosion rocked the van.

"We're sitting ducks here," Frank said. "Come on."

He unbuckled himself, scrambled to the back, and helped Joe up. They tried the van's sliding door, but the impact with the oak tree had jammed it shut. As they moved back to the front of the car, an explosion shattered the rear window inward.

"You know," Joe said, "before this, I always liked bats."

"Looks like they don't like you," Frank said.

The passenger door had been ruined as well, so they gathered at the driver's side exit.

"When we get out, head for the woods," Frank said. "I'm betting that mechanical bats won't be able to deal with trees."

"Let's hope you're right," Joe said. He pushed open the door, and the two of them scrambled for the woods. Fortunately, their car had crashed just scant yards from good tree cover.

Dodging a few dive-bombers, they made it into the forest without further injury. An exploding bat hit a tree near them as they scrambled deeper into the brambles and trees.

"Looks like your plan worked," Joe said as he watched the swarm of bats wheel around the van. Several other bat bombers came at them, but they exploded harmlessly after hitting the trees between the van and the Hardys.

"Out of ammo," Joe said.

"Let's hope," said Frank.

"Think it's safe to go back to the van?" Joe asked.

"Looks like," Frank said. "Let's be careful, though."

The Hardys cautiously left the edge of the woods and went back to their wrecked vehicle.

"I guess we'll be looking for another way home," Joe said. "So much for our safe driver discount."

"Smashed," said Frank, who was walking around the van, making sure the damage was as bad as he thought.

"So, where do we go from here?" Joe asked.

"I'd say we don't have much choice but to carry out our original plan and go back to the mansion—on foot. Let's see what we can salvage."

Fortunately, the Hardys' backpacks had survived the accident largely unscathed. But before they could rummage further, a growl from the nearby woods caught their attention.

"Don't look now," Joe said, "but Fuzzy's back."

Sure enough, the gray form of the wolf-dog loped out of the underbrush near the van. His fangs were bared and a murderous glint lit his yellow eyes. The brothers could hear a faint bird-like whistling as Scavenger approached: Regina Cross giving long-distance orders to her pet.

"Shoo, Scavenger! Shoo!" Joe said, waving his backpack at the animal.

"That didn't work with the spider, Joe. Why do you think it's going to work with Scavenger?"

"We didn't know the spider's name," Joe said. "And it was mechanical, besides."

"Somehow, I don't think being on a first-name basis is going to help," Frank said. "Come on, we don't want him to trap us in the van."

The woods they had crashed into were on the outskirts of Sullivan's Point. Nearby, several small outbuildings loomed out of the late afternoon shadows, and beyond them, the main buildings and weed-dotted streets of the town.

At first the Hardys backed slowly away from Scavenger. The wolf-dog ambled patiently forward, as if waiting for a signal to attack.

When they neared the first buildings, Frank looked at Joe and gave his brother a silent nod. Instantly, the siblings split and ran in opposite directions; Joe for the main street, Frank for the alley running in back of the nearby buildings.

With a growl, Scavenger leapt after Frank. Frank had been on the track team in school, but he knew he couldn't outdistance a wolf for long. His only chance lay in losing the wolf in the streets of Sullivan's Point.

The growling grew louder and Frank risked a glance back. Scavenger had closed the gap between them. A nearby rain barrel gave Frank the chance he needed. Lashing out with his foot as he ran, Frank kicked the barrel into the wolf's path.

The move caught Scavenger by surprise. The barrel hit the animal and tripped him up. He yelped and Frank opened the distance between them.

Frank knew that Joe would be looking for a way to get them out of their predicament, and he hoped that he'd bought his brother enough time to come up with something good.

But when he turned into an alley, his heart sank. In front of him, a wall of boards rose to a height of ten feet. The alley was a dead end.

Knowing he didn't have time to turn back, Frank sprinted toward the fence and jumped. The skills he'd learned on Bayport High's basketball team served him well, and he easily caught the top edge with his fingers. He began to pull himself up just as Scavenger rounded the corner.

The wolf leapt at Frank as he bellied up over the top of the wall. The animal gnashed his teeth and growled; Frank could feel Scavenger's hot breath on his heels. Then the elder Hardy was over the wall and out of harm's way.

He met up with Joe on the other side.

"Lose him?" Joe asked.

Frank shook his head. "Not for long."

"Okay," Joe said, "follow me. I scoped the place out while the wolf chased you." He led Frank into the first floor of a nearby abandoned shop. The sign out front read, Denning & Hayday, Fine Reading. Inside the bookshop was filled with huge, floor-to-ceiling bookshelves, all empty. A winding wooden stairway led to a second floor balcony in the back of the store. A skylight above the balcony provided the store with ample light, even in the late afternoon.

A rolling ladder leaned against the long bookshelf to the right of the doorway. It was tall enough to reach the upper bookshelves.

"Frank," Joe said, "block the stairway with one of those bookcases, then hustle up to the second floor and get ready to leave by the skylight."

"What are you going to do?"

Joe smiled. "See if this wolf is smart enough to open a door."

Frank did as he was told, hiking up to the second floor and pushing a big oak table under the skylight. Joe rolled the ladder toward the front of the store and then took up a position beside the open door. He didn't have to wait long.

Just a minute later Scavenger came bounding down the street, following Frank's scent.

"Hey, hairy! In here!" Joe called.

The wolf turned on a dime and bolted toward the doorway. As he did, Joe scurried up to the top of the ladder.

Scavenger entered the bookshop. As he did, Joe kicked the door with his toe; it slammed shut behind the wolf and locked automatically, just as Joe had planned. Scavenger snarled at Joe and tried to jump up the ladder, but the younger Hardy remained just out of the wolf's reach.

Joe held on to the ladder with both hands, put his feet against the wall above the door, and shoved with all his might. The ladder shot down the wall of bookshelves, stopping only when it hit the balcony railing. Joe hopped off onto the second floor.

Enraged, Scavenger raced for the second floor. But the bookshelves that Frank had toppled at the bottom of the stairs were too high; the wolf couldn't jump over them.

"Great work, Joe!" Frank said as he helped his brother scramble up the table and out of the skylight. Soon, they were on the roof of the building and climbing down a fire escape to street level.

"That ought to hold him," Joe said. "Unless he decides to go through the plate-glass window in the front of the store."

The Hardys looked around. At the end of the street, at the top of the hill, sat the old mansion. One light still shone from the topmost tower room.

"Come on," Frank said. "That's got to be where Cross is holed up. And, with any luck, we'll find Royal there, too." The two of them jogged off in that direction through the shadow-filled alley.

"You know, the mansion is probably filled with booby traps," Joe said. "We really should have gotten a list from Chelsea of all the monsters and pitfalls that she remembers being in the new game."

"I guess we'll just have to count on your experience with the first two games to see us through," Frank said.

"Yeah, but that won't warn us of stuff like the exploding bats. That's from the fourth game—the one that's not out yet. What other stuff did Chelsea say was in A Town Called Chaos?"

Frank thought for a minute as they jogged. Ahead of them loomed a huge, shabby-looking warehouse.

"The bats, the driverless car, the ghost of Katherine Chaos's evil sister, a mansion full of traps, and . . ."

Suddenly the ground around them shook and the roof of the old warehouse exploded into a thousand splinters of wood. A huge shape rose up out of the wreckage, its humanlike torso two stories tall. The hairy monstrosity threw back its head and bellowed its rage to the twilight sky.

"A giant ape!" Frank cried.

# 14 The Ghost in the Mansion

"Duck!" yelled Joe.

The Hardys hit the pavement as a huge hairy fist whooshed over their heads, slamming into the side of a nearby building. The giant ape howled angrily.

"This can't be happening!" Joe said.

"Right now, I don't think we have time to argue with reality," Frank said as he got to his feet.

The ape's other fist came smashing down. Joe rolled to one side, while Frank jumped to the other. The fist hit the ground between the brothers with a thunderous boom. The ape gazed down at the Hardys, its red eyes blazing like lasers.

As Frank and Joe turned and ran toward the mansion, a giant hand crashed down in front of them, cutting them off. They turned and ran back the way they had come. The fist hit the side of another building, sending splinters of wood raining down on the brothers. The monster roared.

"This isn't working," Joe yelled.

"I know," Frank said. "But we have to keep moving or we'll be pancakes." As he spoke, the fist crashed down in front of them once again.

"Let's split up," Joe said. "It can't get us both at once."

"Actually," Frank said, "it's having trouble getting us at all. If you notice it just keeps doing the same things over and over."

Frank dodged and Joe ducked as the fist went by again. "You're right!" Joe said. "It's not acting intelligently at all." He looked at the ape's giant face. Its eyes flashed, its mouth opened and shut, it roared. "That's why it hasn't turned us into pulp yet. It's not as sophisticated as Cross's other mechanical creatures."

"Probably she didn't have the money to construct something this big from scratch," Frank said. "We're looking at Giganto, unless I miss my guess. Remember the amusement park on the way into town? But just because it was part of a thrill ride doesn't make it any less dangerous."

"I think it homes in on our movements," Joe said. "It's got some kind of a motion sensor. And it hasn't moved out of that old warehouse to chase us."

Frank nodded as they dodged the swinging fist once more. "I don't think it can," he said. "I doubt it even has the lower part of its body. The power source must be in that warehouse. If you can keep it distracted, I'll try to get into the warehouse and shut it down."

"Just don't take too long," Joe said. "I'm starting to feel like that girl in *King Kong* already."

Frank spotted a boarded-up door in the wall of the warehouse nearby. "Try to draw it to the other end of the alley," he called to Joe.

Joe nodded and took off. Frank pressed himself against the nearest wall and stood motionless. The ape's red eyes locked on Joe and the fist followed. Frank sprinted to the door and gave it his best karate kick.

The boards broke, but not enough to let him in. He kicked again. Out of the corner of his eye, he could see Joe down the alleyway, playing dodgeball with the giant fist. "Make it quick, will you?" the younger Hardy called to his brother.

The third kick made a large enough hole, and Frank pushed his way into the warehouse. Sure enough, the torso of the ape was connected to a huge mass of cables and wires inside the warehouse. Lights blinked on what Frank assumed must be a control panel.

He dashed to the panel, made a quick assessment of it, and then pulled on a large relay cable.

Immediately the ape's movements slowed. Its red eyes stopped flashing, and its roar wound down like the sound of a tape player when its batteries have suddenly gone dead. Joe came through the door as the giant ape ground to a halt.

"Thanks," he said, wiping sweat from his forehead. "That's about all the workout I need for today."

"If you'd remembered to put the giant bananas in your backpack, this wouldn't have been a problem," Frank said.

Joe smiled. "Let's go get Regina Cross."

Frank nodded. The two of them left the warehouse and sprinted up the hill to the mansion. The house wasn't in much better repair than the rest of the town. It was a huge shell of a place with columns beside the entrance and gables on the roof. One solitary tower stretched above the roofline, but the light inside it—which the Hardys had seen previously—was out.

Despite its dilapidated appearance, the mansion did sport a new mat on the doorstep emblazoned with the word *Welcome* in bright red letters. As Frank and Joe studied the entryway, they heard a crash from somewhere back in the village.

"What do you think that was?" Frank asked.

"I think probably old Scavenger decided to go through that window after all," Joe said. They could hear the strange whistling again, which seemed to be coming from the tower of the house.

"Then let's get inside and out of his range," Frank said. "Maybe we can stop that whistling, too. I'd bet Cross has a loudspeaker up in that tower. Taking it out might slow Scavenger." He was about to turn the doorknob when Joe stopped him.

"Wait," Joe said. "In School of Chaos most of the doors were booby-trapped." He pushed aside the doormat with his foot. Under it, the porch showed a suspicious seam. Carefully avoiding that spot, Joe opened the door.

Where the mat had been, a trapdoor opened. Frank and Joe looked into the hole but couldn't see the bottom. They stepped around it, entered the house, and closed the door behind them.

"That was in the second game?" Frank asked.

Joe nodded. "Yeah. Now that I think of it, we haven't run into *any* traps that weren't in the first two games—or the upcoming one. Nothing from the third game. Not even Bombo Bear. I wonder why?"

"Maybe Cross only wants to use game elements that her family worked on," Frank said.

"Could be that ties into the 'My past is the key to the future' clue," Joe said.

Frank knitted his brow and said, "Hmm."

"What is it?" Joe asked.

"I just had an idea about Regina Cross," Frank said. "Where to, now?"

"Either up or down," Joe said. "Prisoners are always kept in the tower or the dungeon."

Just at that moment, the grandfather clock at the far end of the hall struck thirteen.

"Duck!" Joe shouted.

The Hardys ducked just as the clock face popped open and its hands shot down the corridor like arrows. They thunked harmlessly into the frame of the door.

"Thanks for the warning," Frank said.

Joe nodded. "School of Chaos had deadly clocks. Made recess interesting. So, up or down?"

"I'm betting that the light in the tower was a red herring," Frank said. "The whistling probably is, too, come to think of it. Let's see if we can find a way down."

The brothers cautiously searched the first floor of the mansion. "If we can find the kitchen," Frank said, "we can probably find the cellar door. Most old houses used the cellar for cold food storage."

"Well, we won't be using our noses to find the kitchen," Joe said. "Smells like all Regina Cross has been cooking in here is mildew. She really needs to get a better housekeeper."

They avoided an electrified rug in the living room and eventually made their way to the back of the house and the kitchen. Sure enough, one door in the kitchen opened onto a long descending staircase. Frank found a light switch and turned it on.

The stairs led down to a flagstone floor some twenty feet below. "Hold on to the railings," Joe said. "I have a bad feeling about these stairs."

He and Frank gripped the railings tightly as they went down the stairs. Good thing, too, because when they were halfway down, the stairs flattened under them and turned into a steep ramp. The Hardys' feet slipped out from under them, but their grip on the rails kept them from sliding into the pit that opened up at the bottom of the slide.

Using their arms like gymnasts on the parallel bars, they edged down the railings and then jumped off the sides near the bottom, landing on either side of the pit. Frank looked down into the hole. "Spikes at the bottom," he said. "Nasty. Our hostess plays rough."

"No wonder she doesn't have many visitors," Joe said.

They could hear some muffled sounds coming from beyond a door in the cellar's far wall. The

Hardys opened the door cautiously, first checking to make sure that no trapdoors would open under them. But as the door swung open, a cobra sprang out.

Frank and Joe jumped back. "Mechanical?" Frank asked. The six-foot snake seemed focused on him, its head weaving back and forth slightly.

"I hope so," Joe said. He darted forward, grabbed the snake by the tail, and whipped its head against the cellar wall. Sure enough, sparks flew and the snake fell limp in his hands, wires hanging from where its head had been.

"Snake charmers have nothing on you," Frank said.

Joe nodded. "Let's see who's behind this door." Cautiously, the brothers stepped into the room. It was a plain chamber, with a flagstone floor and stone walls. Only one door, the door they came through, led from the room. In the center of the room sat a man tied to a chair. The man appeared to be of medium height and build and had a full beard and long brown hair. He had a gag in his mouth.

When he saw the Hardys, the man started bouncing up and down in the chair and making the muffled cries the Hardys had heard from outside. Joe dropped the snake at the man's feet and used his pocketknife to cut the ropes on the man's legs; Frank freed the man's upper body. As the ropes fell away from his hands, the man pulled the gag from his mouth.

"You must be Steven Royal," Joe said, still working on the lower ropes.

"She's crazy!" he said. "She was going to kill me!"

As he said it, a growl from behind them made the Hardys spin. A panel had opened in the far wall and through it stepped a thin blond woman with dark glasses. At her side loped Scavenger, the half-wolf. She had a loaded repeating cross-bow in her hands. The bow was leveled at the Hardys, and she held the wolf by the scruff of the neck to keep it in check.

Joe, still crouched at the foot of the chair, cut the last of Royal's ropes and said, "Regina Cross, I presume."

# 15 Double Cross

The woman in the doorway nodded and almost smiled. Scavenger growled at the Hardys and prepared to spring.

"Actually, she's not Regina Cross at all," Frank said. "There is no Regina Cross. There never was. Isn't that right, Ms. Sakai?"

Joe whistled. "Of course!"

"So," she said, taking off her dark glasses, "you figured out my little secret. I'm impressed." She pulled off her blond wig as well and shook loose her long black hair. Anne Sakai dropped the wig and glasses to the floor. Slim and athletic, she looked like a video-game heroine come to life.

"The clues were all there," Frank said, "but your apparent death kept us from figuring it out too soon. But what Joe said about there being no traps from the third game and 'My past is the future' helped me figure it out. You didn't work on that game, but you did work on the first two *and* the new one.

"That made me realize that we'd been misunderstanding part of the riddles," Frank continued. "If Royal wasn't running this game, then it couldn't be *his* past the riddles referred to. And there was only one other person who had a history with the Chaos series—you. Joe was right about your not wanting to use anything from a game you hadn't worked on."

"Call it vanity," Sakai said, her voice tinged with sweet venom. "But I just never much liked the work of second-rate hacks. Especially on *my* project."

"That's why you sent the wolf after us in the forest, rather than a bear," Joe said, still bent over. As he spoke, his hand found the remains of the mechanical snake on the floor. He tightened his fist around its tail.

"The bear was a joke," Sakai said. "And a bad one at that. That whole game was a joke, wasn't it, Steven?"

Royal turned red. "It was a good game!" he said. "It's not my fault if the public didn't like it."

"The public didn't like it because *I* was the heart and soul of the Chaos series," Sakai said, fixing Royal with an icy stare. "You were nothing without me."

"Well, you were nothing without me, either," Royal said. He started to step forward, but a growl from Scavenger changed his mind. "That's why you came crawling back to work on A Town Called Chaos."

"There was no Town Called Chaos before I contacted you," Sakai said. "And there wouldn't be one without me—and there *won't* be."

"Royal cut you out of the jackpot, didn't he?" Frank said, trying to keep her talking. "He'd made sure that he controlled who got paid when the game finally came out."

"After all the work I did . . ." Sakai said, smoldering.

"Ha!" Royal said. "You didn't do any work on Chaos Three, but I still paid money to your estate—or rather *you*—for it. It's only fair that I get that money back on the new game. I paid you for the work you've already done, but I won't share the profits. It's only fair."

"Doesn't seem fair to me," Joe said, slowly standing. He had the snake in his hand but was careful to keep it hidden behind his body as he stood.

"So, why'd you do it?" Frank asked, drawing Sakai's attention back to himself. "Why did you fake your own death?"

"Tax trouble," Sakai said. "And fans who just wouldn't leave me alone. When that McLean woman found me in the Caribbean, I knew that I had to drop out of sight permanently. If she could find me so easily, the IRS would have no trouble. And I owed them big time."

She seemed to enjoy telling her story, so Frank and Joe let her go on. They exchanged a secret glance, hoping Royal would keep his big mouth shut for a while.

"But with me 'dead' and the money in a Swiss account . . . problem solved." She smiled.

"How'd you pull it off," Joe asked. "It must have been tricky."

"Child's play," Sakai said. "For someone with my computer skills, creating a new identity was easy. Amazing what a passport computer will do if you just know how to ask it. The plane crash wasn't any harder. I parachuted out long before the plane hit and then rafted back to the island where I assumed my new life as Regina Cross."

"McLean saw you," Frank said. "But she assumed you were a ghost."

"She's never been very stable," Sakai said, smiling.

"Neither have you!" Royal said. He was nervous and sweating profusely.

For a moment it seemed as though Sakai would shoot him on the spot. Then Joe said, "I disagree.

You've got to be pretty together to pull off all of this. What I want to know, though, is why you decided to do another game."

Sakai frowned. "The money ran out. I'd spent a lot of it buying what's left of this town and the local amusement park. And living in Switzerland wasn't cheap, either. That's why I gave it up and moved home. The only thing Cross Enterprises has left there is a computer hookup in a one-room flat.

"Plus"—and here her eyes narrowed angrily again—"I didn't get as much money from Chaos Three as I thought I would."

"You shouldn't have gotten any at all," Royal said. "You didn't actually work on the game."

"But I created the series," she said. "That entitled me to my cut. And then you had the gall to try to cut me out of this one as well."

"A dead woman would have had a hard time going to court to collect, I imagine," Frank said. "Is that why you did it, Royal?"

"Yes . . . No! She owed it to m-me," Royal stammered.

"You see why I had no trouble luring him up here," Sakai said to the Hardys. "Greedy and vain, through and through. His only real talent is self-promotion. You know, I was happy in Switzerland. If Forest of Chaos hadn't been such a flop, I would never have come back—except to see my

Scavenger." She scratched the wolfdog behind the ears and whistled. The animal barked and stared up at her.

"Did you know I picked the town in Switzerland where I lived because it was near where Ian Tochi grew up?" she asked Royal. "He told such wonderful stories about the place. He was right about it, too. But Switzerland, just over the border, was better for me because of my—tax situation."

She sighed nostalgically. "Such a nice guy, Tochi. He had *way* more talent than you, Steven. I should have hooked up with *him* as a partner."

As she spoke, Frank got a good grip on the back of the chair Royal had been tied to. He and Joe exchanged glances.

Sakai smiled a cold smile. "Maybe I *will* hook up with him after this," she said. "See, I had planned to ruin Steven's reputation and then let him go. I'd assume a new identity and start over again; no one would ever believe him. Such an absurd story. Now, however, I'm afraid I'll have to kill you all."

# 16 The Final Blow

Sakai's finger tightened on the trigger of the crossbow.

Before she could pull it, though, Joe lashed out, using the mechanical snake like a whip. The snake smashed into the crossbow, yanking it from Sakai's hands. Joe brought the snake back on the rebound, hitting Sakai in the ribs. She gasped in pain and surprise and staggered to one side.

Scavenger leapt forward to protect his mistress, but Frank was ready for him. The elder Hardy, moving like a lion tamer, shoved the chair that Royal had been tied to into the wolf's face. Scavenger tried to bite Frank through the chair. Frank pushed the chair and twisted, trapping the wolf's head between the chair's legs.

Scavenger yelped and jumped in the air, trying to get the chair off. The back of the chair came off in Frank's hand. Frank gave the seat of the chair a shove with his foot and the wolf skidded into a corner of the room. He sat there, yelping and trying to get his head out of his wooden prison.

Before the Hardys could stop her, Sakai picked up the crossbow and fired.

Frank whipped the chair back in front of his chest and the arrow thonked into it. He flung the wooden fragment at Sakai before she could fire again. It hit her and she fell backward.

Moving quickly, Frank and Joe yanked Royal through the secret panel Sakai had used to enter the room.

For a frantic moment Joe looked around. Then he reached up and pulled a lever to one side of the door. The secret panel swung shut. A crossbow bolt thudded into the closed door.

"Chaos Two," Joe said by way of explanation. "A lot of the doors in that game were operated by levers." He took the mechanical snake and jammed its remains against the bottom of the panel as a doorstop. "That should keep her from following us, at least for a while," he said.

At the end of the secret passage, the three of them found a spiral staircase leading up. They took it. The stairway led to another secret panel that emptied into the mansion's library.

"I don't know how to thank you guys," Royal said.

"Just keep quiet until we're out of this mess," Frank said.

"I hear footsteps," Joe said. "Looks like we didn't slow her down for long."

Frank picked up a leather-backed library chair and threw it through one of the big windows of the room. "Everybody out!" he said.

They hustled Royal out the window first and then followed. Frank brought up the rear. As the elder Hardy's feet hit the uncut lawn outside, a crossbow bolt whizzed over his head. "Keep running," he called to Joe and Royal.

Royal stumbled as they reached the street. Frank and Joe had to pull him up and, as they did, Sakai put a crossbow bolt into Joe's backpack.

"Joe!" yelled Frank.

"I'm okay!" Joe said. "It didn't get through the pack."

They ran into the town, trying to put buildings between them and the deadly crossbow. They darted down alleys and cut through deserted structures, dragging Royal with them. Every time they thought it was safe to catch a breather, another crossbow bolt would whiz by.

"She knows this town better than we do,"

Frank said, panting. "We need to come up with a plan."

"I've got an idea," said Joe. "With a little luck, we can take her out."

A few minutes later Joe rounded a corner and came face-to-face with Sakai. She fired at him, but he ducked back and the arrow hit a building. Joe took off at top speed, angling for the old warehouse. He knew that sooner or later she'd hit him if he gave her many more chances.

Sure enough, another shot whizzed by just as he turned into the alley behind the warehouse. Giganto loomed high overhead, mute witness to the deadly chase. But as Joe reached the far end of the alley he tripped. He looked back the way he'd come.

Anne Sakai came around the corner walking slowly, like a hunter closing in on her prey. She took careful aim at Joe as he lay in the alley.

"Now, Frank! Now!" Joe yelled.

"Now, Frank! Now!" Sakai repeated mockingly, closing the distance between them for a better shot.

Just at that instant, Giganto sprang to life. The ape bellowed his rage and his fist came crashing down. Sakai looked up, too late to get out of the way. The ape's fist grazed her with enough force to crush her to the ground. The crossbow slipped from Sakai's hand as she lay unconscious.

Joe breathed a sigh of relief. The ape stopped moving. Frank and Royal stepped out of the warehouse.

"Good thing you got that relay cable fixed when you did," Joe said to Frank. "Another minute and I'd have been shishkebab."

"Hey, I've always been as good at fixing things as breaking them," Frank said, smiling.

Royal looked overjoyed. "You did it! You got her!" he said.

Joe got up and dusted himself off. "Oh no," he said. "We didn't get her. 'Twas the beast that felled the beauty."

A day later the Hardys found themselves back in the offices of Viking Software.

It hadn't taken them long to find Sakai's SUV behind the mansion. They tied up the woman and sat her in the back of her car. Then they went back to the basement and locked Scavenger in the room where Royal had been held. The wolf proved no trouble this time. Struggling to escape from the chair had exhausted him.

After securing the bad guys, the Hardys and Royal hightailed it back to Benson. Once there, they turned Sakai over to the local police and called the SPCA to deal with Scavenger. Then they—and Royal—spent a long night explaining the whole adventure to the cops.

Royal returned with them to Jewel Ridge, but decided to take a long vacation after turning over the real master game disk to the Hardys. He'd had the disk on him when Sakai captured him. She had told him to bring it when she lured him to Sullivan's Point. She claimed she'd found a major bug in the program.

Fortunately, the Hardys and Royal had found the disk when they searched the mansion for Sakai's car keys. It had been in the topmost tower, along with Sakai's computer and the keys.

"Of course," Joe said to Chelsea, Phil, and Dave, "there was no bug in the game. But Royal hadn't done enough of the programming to be sure. Looks like Sakai really *was* the brains of that partnership."

"And, as we suspected, Sakai did have her own program within the university computer. When we went poking around, the program activated, sending us the clue. That's how she knew when to go to Kendall State Park with Scavenger and roll the rocks away from the cave entrance," Frank said.

"I bet she has taps in the company system, as well," Phil said. "She probably knew every move we made as we were making it. We'll have to do a careful sweep to make sure we've got all of Sakai's bugs out of the Viking computers."

"So sad," Chelsea said. "To waste all that talent on a game of revenge."

"I'm not sure that Royal didn't deserve at least some of what he got," Phil said. "It's just too bad that the rest of you got dragged into it."

"I talked to our lawyers and they said they think that they can sort this mess out," Dave said. "It may take a while, but Viking Software can hang on until then. And the publicity from all this will make A Town Called Chaos an instant best-seller."

"Just as long as they keep Sakai in jail for a long time," said Joe.

"I don't think there's any doubt about that," Frank said. "She's still got tax troubles, she faked her own death and forged a passport, she kidnapped Royal, plus she tried to kill us. I'm sure she broke a half-dozen other laws as well. The police will probably give Royal a good looking over, too. Maybe they'll scare some sense into him."

Joe smiled. "Couldn't happen to a nicer guy. I know you Viking guys need his game to succeed, but he really is a jerk."

"Jerk, genius," Dave said, shrugging. "Sometimes the two go together."

"Present company excepted," Phil said, and they all laughed.

"You know," Chelsea said, "this whole adventure has given me an idea for a game of my own. Maybe you guys could play-test it."

"Just so long as it doesn't have any wolves," Frank said.

"Or giant apes," added Joe.

"A giant ape?" Chelsea said. "I think that's been done to death."